D1798156

Sex Gets In The Way

For John Perkins

John Haylock

Sex Gets In The Way

A

ARCADIA BOOKS
LONDON

Arcadia Books Ltd.
15-16 Nassau Street
London W1W 7AB

www.arcadiabooks.co.uk

First published in the United Kingdom in 2006 by Arcadia Books
Copyright © John Haylock 2006

John Haylock has asserted his moral right to be identified as the
author of this work in accordance with the Copyright, Designs and Patents Act, 1988.

A catalogue record for this book is available from the British Library.

ISBN 1-905147-01-5

Typeset in Bembo by Basement Press - London
Printed in Finland

Arcadia Books supports English PEN, the fellowship of writers who work together to promote
literature and its understanding. English PEN upholds writers' freedoms in Britain and around
the world, challenging political and cultural limits on free expression.
To find out more, visit www.englishpen.org or contact
English PEN, 6-8 Amwell Street, London EC1R 1UQ.

Arcadia Books distributors are as follows:

in the UK and elsewhere in Europe:
Turnaround Publishers Services
Unit 3, Olympia Trading Estate Coburg Road London N22 6TZ

in the USA and Canada:
Independent Publishers Group
814 N. Franklin St. Chicago, IL 60610

in Australia:
Tower Books
PO Box 213 Brookvale, NSW 2100

in New Zealand:
Addenda
Box 78224 Grey Lynn Auckland

in South Africa:
Quartet Sales and Marketing
PO Box 1218 Northcliffe Johannesburg 2115

Arcadia Books is the *Sunday Times* Small Publisher of the Year

Part I

Twenty minutes before teatime in late October 1928 Dr Stephen Lambert opened his eyes and, from his winged armchair, surveyed his wife, who, seated at her escritoire near the far end of the long drawing-room, was penning a letter in her neat hand.

'Who are you writing to?'

'Florence.'

Dr Lambert did not like his wife's first cousin; it displeased him that she was regarded as an aunt by his only child, James, now aged ten. 'Well, I suppose I'd better take the dogs out.'

'As you wish, darling.'

Slowly, Dr Lambert rose. He was a tall man of fifty-eight; his thin receding hair gave him a high forehead, although like many practitioners of general medicine, he was far from being an intellectual. 'Anything for the post?'

'Not yet.'

'D'you want me to wait?'

'I'll take it myself.' Mrs Lambert liked to preserve some independence.

Dr Lambert harnessed his wife's cairn terrier to a lead, which he took down from its hook in the porch and outside the house he attached another lead to the collar of a Dalmatian eagerly waiting by the kennel for his walk. With the reluctant cairn tugging one arm back and the willing Dalmatian pulling the other arm forward, Stephen James Lambert, P.R.C.S., L.R.C.P., ('The Doctor' as his servants and some of his patients called him) ambled down the drive of Gorsebanks, through the high

1

wooden gates and then up the road to the seafront. Once on the cliffs, he released the Dalmatian, who sprang frolicking ahead. The cairn could not be let off the lead, otherwise ears back, eyes popping, she would bolt straight home to his wife.

Sudden squalls loosed bursts of rain; the doctor pulled on the peak of his Harris Tweed cap and fastened the top button of his mackintosh. The undulating cliff paths were empty and only an occasional motorcar or van passed along the Overcliff Drive. Swanage and the Isle of Wight were invisible: the yellow flanks of Mengistbury Head simmered in the east, while Boscombe and Bournemouth piers were dark fingers in the west. The doctor walked slowly, thinking about Mrs Rothwell, the richest of his twenty odd patients, who might at this moment be watching him from her bay-windowed bedroom in the Island View Hotel. She spent much of her day gazing out to sea with a novel on her lap. Although Dr Lambert had prescribed champagne and drives in a closed car, she confined herself to the former regimen, imbibing larger doses than the 'dear doctor' had intended, to the satisfaction of the hotel management.

Mrs Rothwell was no beauty, having a blotched, swollen face and scanty white hair, but the experience of life and her money had imbued her with an ease of manner and a sophistication that Dr Lambert found pleasing. His visits to her lasted longer than those to the other patients on his brief but profitable list.

The Dalmatian bounded ahead only pausing to sniff at and then raise his leg against a clump of marran grass. He chose a shelter for his next convenience and on arrival barked. Was someone there? Perhaps lovers were indulging.

'Come here at once!' cried Dr Lambert. The Dalmatian gambolled away. The doctor dragged the cairn to the shelter. Inside, stretched out full length on the bench seat was Bessie Harlow, the Bannerman-Wright's cook. Unkempt, clothes shabby, her felt hat askew, she seemed down and out. His eyes were shut. Dr Lambert dropped the cairn's lead and felt her pulse and slapped her cheek. She opened her eyes. 'Doctor!'

She was not only heavily pregnant but badly ill. She sat up, her head between her hands and wept. 'Oh, excuse me, sir. I'm all done in. I have nowhere to go. I don't know what to do.'

'Stay where you are, Bessie. You'll be all right. I'll fetch my motor.

The cairn, free, had run home dragging her lead. Dr Lambert captured the Dalmatian and strode back to Gorsebanks. He realised that Bessie was in such a grave state that she might not survive, but it was his duty to try and save her and if not her then the child that was soon to be born.

*

'Is there absolutely no one, no one at all she knew, no relation of any kind?' Mrs Lambert asked her husband.

'Mrs Bannerman-Wright got her from an orphanage when she was seventeen and trained her. She became quite a good cook. There was a sister who went to Canada or somewhere, but no one knows where she is. All we know of the father is that his name was Henry. Mrs Bannerman-Wright saw him once in the kitchen with Bessie on his lap and ordered him out of the house. Later when her condition was discovered she sacked her.'

'Stephen…' Margaret began. She was sitting opposite her husband on the other side of the coal and wood fire in the drawing room, now, for the sake of warmth, divided in half by crimson velvet curtains. 'Stephen, we must adopt the baby.'

The doctor lowered *The Times* and sighed. 'It would be as unfair to the infant as to James. Inevitably we would favour our own, how could we not? The child would grow up feeling he didn't belong...'

'We could give him our affection, our love, our name, even.'

'But could you give him the same affection you give to James?'

'We could try, Stephen, we could try.'

'I would not want to play the part of father to a child born in the gutter; his breeding or lack of it would show.'

Mrs Lambert sighed at her husband's snobbish unchristian attitude; she would have voted Socialist if the doctor had not been a die-hard Tory.

'I know what you're thinking, Margaret. I'm not mean or unphilanthropic. I'm simply a realist. However much we tried to treat him as our own child he would never really be ours; at the back of our minds, at the back of his. It's better for him to grow up with his own kind.'

'But where?'

'In a home with other orphans.'

'Poor little baby. Which home?'

'A church home, conveniently far, in Eastbourne. An Anglo-catholic home with a Father Hopkins in charge and a matron, an ex-nurse. The place is like a private home. There are only fourteen boys.'

'That doesn't sound so bad.' Margaret Lambert leant forward in her armchair.

'Stephen, let us be his godparents, if nothing else; that would give him some sort of background. When he grows up he can come and stay here. James will be a man and out in the world. What will they baptise him?'

'The mother asked that he be called Henry Gordon before she died. He'll take his mother's surname.'

'What did his father do?'

'According to Mrs Bannerman-Wright he cannot be traced. There were no letters among Bessie's things.'

The doctor raised *The Times* again, pushed up his spectacles and muttered, 'Can't even be sure what he travelled in, whether it was shoes, shirts or sausages; it evidently wasn't rubber goods.'

Mrs Lambert frowned and went on with her library book.

*

James was not told about his mother's godson. Dr Lambert had declined the doubtful honour of being a godparent. He was afraid that connection with the orphan boy might arouse jealousy in James; there was the problem of explaining how someone like Henry had come into the world. Mrs Lambert was not sure of the jealousy idea. 'If we had another child James might be jealous of a baby brother or sister.'

'That wouldn't be the same,' insisted the doctor. 'It's a question of breeding, not of environment. Breeding comes out. Good environment cannot eradicate bad breeding. Think of your dog's pedigree.'

Mrs Lambert was no snob, though she admitted to herself, and was ashamed to do so, that she would be mortified if James married a shop-girl.

When the time came for the orphan to be baptised the boy was at the home in Eastbourne. Mrs Lambert kept her promise to be a godmother, although her husband dissuaded her from attending the ceremony.

Father Hopkins added Henry to his list of godsons. The other godmother was Mrs Barnes, the home nurse.

4

Mrs Lambert sent Henry a silver christening mug, but Father Hopkins said he would look after it, as it was too valuable to have 'knocking about the home'. Henry never saw it or knew it existed.

While Henry, the bastard, cried and wailed, soiled his nappies and learnt to say 'Fa-fa' and 'Ba-Ba' to his surrogate father, the Rev. Martin Hopkins MA (Cantab.) and his foster mother, Mrs Winifred Barnes SRN, James, the sole heir of Dr and Mrs Stephen Lambert, was being taught French and Latin, history and mathematics, singing and drawing and other useful subjects and wholesome games at a local preparatory school, unaware of the advantage of being legitimate.

James often felt lonely. When upstairs in his own sitting room at Gorsebanks he would ponder over his circumstances and wish they were different. How dull it was to be English! To belong to all that red on the map. He yearned to belong to some other land, somewhere exotic. If only he were Chinese. For a while he would go about with his eyes half-closed trying to look oriental. 'Stop that, James,' his mother would say, 'you look silly.'

*

Mr Tupper the Lambert's vicar, was a bachelor. A band of wealthy widows and gushing spinsters put themselves under his command. Miss Ursula Reynolds, a first cousin of Dr Lambert, ensured that Mr Tupper's Easter offering reached four figures. His Puseyite church was built in 1882 when the seaside village was starting to develop into a small resort for those like Dr Lambert who came from yeomen stock or for those whose fortunes derived from commerce. The inhabitants liked to think that their move from London or the Midlands benefited themselves and at the same time helped to create an exclusive haven away from the rapidly spreading towns of Boscombe and Bournemouth which had already begun to suffer from the vulgarity that development brings.

A good proportion of the newcomers when they were anything were Methodists and a few of them heard the vicar's sermons delivered at Sung Eucharist. Mr Tupper or Father Tupper as he soon became, was more intellectual than most of his parishioners; he would preach for half an hour or more. Ursula Reynolds dutifully took down the sermons in a shorthand invented by herself; at times she could not decipher her code much to the annoyance of the vicar, who liked to publish his extempore ramblings in the parish magazine.

A change was taking place at the church. Father Tupper, after the prayer of consecration, which he would mumble inaudibly, would beat his breast and cry *'nobis quoique peccatoribus'*. Miss Reynolds presented a statue of the Madonna and Child, which would have looked more at home in a Spanish church; placed in front of a pillar half way up the nave, it formed a Shrine of Our Lady. A large crucifix was hung above the chancel steps and referred to proudly by some as 'our rood screen'. 'Positively spikey,' Miss Simpson-Cox, a friend of Mrs Lambert's said delightedly in her resonant baritone. Her father, a philatelist of some repute and a possessor of a considerable fortune, a Van Dyck beard and a trenchant tongue, left the church-going to his daughter, who enjoyed a kind of flirtation with Rome. 'She goes to church so often she makes up for my absence,' he said once to Dr Lambert. When Mr Simpson-Cox heard about the installation of the holy statue he scandalised his daughter by calling it 'Our Lady of the Teacups.' 'Oh Father, how can you!' 'But isn't it true,' he chortled, 'that Ursula Reynolds had a vision during one of her tea parties and was commanded by the Virgin Tupper to put up an image?'

In 1928, the year of Henry Harlow's birth, the congregation of the church attended by the Lamberts was not very different from what it had been in 1908 when the doctor and his wife had settled in the parish. There was Mr Dent, the chemist, who was a sideman and respectful to Dr Lambert, his social superior and valued customer; Mr Avery, the verger, with a tousled head, a brindled tuft under his nose that made him appear mouthless, a stoop and a limp won in the Great War; his younger brother, a taller and more erect version of himself, was the Lambert's gardener and also the local lamplighter of the gas street lamps; and Mr Baker, a teacher at the Church of England school. Mr Baker, whose sleek brown hair was parted in the middle, wore plus fours, played the organ and trained the choir composed of shopkeepers and their sons. 'Mr Baker is wonderful with the boys,' cooed the parish ladies. 'He gives up so much of his time to them.' The Mr Dents, the Avery brothers, the Mr Bakers and the domestic servants, who depended on their jobs for their livelihood, with their money invested in debentures, preference shares and the funds – no risky, non-dividend paying ordinary shares for them – they did not feel completely secure. How could they with all that industrial strife going on in the Midlands and in the North, that menacing army of the unemployed. Mrs Lambert remembered the less fortunate in her prayers; her husband was more practical: he had meal tickets to give out-of-works who sometimes rang his bell – 'No good giving them money,' he said.

*

St Nicholas's Home for Orphan Boys, where Henry Barlow was installed, came under the wing of the Eastbourne church to which Father Hopkins served as curate. He was as popular with the ladies of the parish as Father Tupper, though his affection for the opposite sex was restricted to those members of it who had passed through the menopause. He got on well with Mrs Barnes (or Barney as the boys called her), the matron of the Home, who was fifty-three; he worked in harmony with the rector, a near millionaire bachelor.

Henry Harlow at three could not be aware of the changes taking place in his parish church, built five years before Father Tupper's. It boasted not only a Lady Chapel, but also a statue of 'Our Lord representing the love which pours out from his Sacred Heart'. In both churches the Blessed Sacrament was now reserved – 'preserved' James thought his mother had said when explaining the innovation.

At thirteen James found church tedious, nevertheless he took the line of least resistance attending the Sung Eucharist on Sundays with his parents, who had already been to the 'eight o'clock', and accepting preparation for confirmation by Father Tupper along with the chemist's son and other local boys. James was the only boy from his prep school in the confirmation class. Mrs Lambert insisted that her son should make his confession before being confirmed. He was given a little red book of peccadilloes and penances: 'I have been selfish,' 'I have told lies,' 'I have been sulky,' ran the list and James wrote them down on a piece of paper as instructed by his mother. 'Afterwards when your slate is clean, you will have a wonderful feeling of relief,' she told him. 'I always put my list down a drain in the road outside the church. You should do the same.' James didn't, nor did he include in his list 'I have committed sins of the flesh' or 'I have practised self-pollution' because he didn't tell Father Tupper, who often came to tea with his parents, that he had masturbated and also done so mutually with the boys in his school dormitory. Tupper was a formidable person to confess such intimacies to. With his tufts of hair poking out of his nostrils and his ears, the strands of black hair mingled with grey protruding from the sides of his beretta, his gold-rimmed spectacles magnifying brown eyes, and his pasty indoor complexion the Father was intimidating.

A few months after his confirmation, which had meant much less to him than his devout mother had hoped, James went to his public school, a medium-low church establishment that did not require its boys to confess. Sexual games were rife and more advanced than at his prep school and James felt no shame in taking part in them. The fear of discovery worried James, but it was less powerful than the urge of the flesh.

*

Five years later James's schooling was over and Henry's had just started. James was in Tours learning French; Henry was singing in the choir.

At Christmas and Easter Mrs Lambert sent Henry presents each accompanied by a holy card, a secular card and parcel were despatched for his birthday. Neither the Home nor Henry acknowledged these gifts. For the first few years Mrs Lambert did not bother about this lack of gratitude, but when in 1938 Henry had reached the age of ten she considered that he was old enough to be able to write a letter of thanks and she wrote to Father Hopkins telling him so.

'My dear Mrs Lambert,

It was indeed a pleasure to hear from the godmother of our beloved Henry. He is growing into a fine lad and is a happy member of our little family. He joined the choir a year or so ago and is learning to serve at the altar, having acted already as an acolyte at High Mass, ringing the sacring bell. He goes to the nearby church along with our other boys at our Home.

This, my dear Mrs Lambert, brings me to the question in your letter. I have written the word with a capital, for, alas, it is a Home and not a home, and unavoidably there is a difference. Some of the boys do not even have someone like your good self interested in them, and therefore it is considered by me as Principal of St Nicholas's and by Father Cyril Willingdon-Russett, our Rector and Chairman, that no boy should be favoured above another, or appear to have an advantage over his 'brothers'. Therefore, when presents arrive, such as those you have so kindly and regularly sent to our Henry, we, following the rules of the Home put them into a pool so that they are shared by all our little sons. Thus we avoid creating a situation whereby any one boy feels he is privileged.

Remembering our Lord's words: "That thy alms may be in secret; and the Father, which seeth is secret himself shall reward them openly".

In future, therefore, dear Mrs Lambert, when you send your parcel – and we are delighted and grateful to receive presents – please address it to me and not specifically to Henry.

May our Lord Jesus Christ's blessing be upon you.

Yours very sincerely.

> Martin Hopkins, M.A.
> (Cantab.),
> Clerk in Holy Orders,
> Principal.'

Mrs Lambert saw Father Hopkins's point and did as required. She believed the Father to be both a good Christian and a fine priest, who sincerely did his best for his charges. Nevertheless to be denied any direct contact with her godson saddened her. Dr Lambert opined that Hopkins was right and that it would be unfair if Henry could boast of a wealthy godparent to his fellow inmates.

'He must remain like the other boys in the Home,' said the doctor. 'To lift him out of his class would only make him wretched in the end.'

Mrs Lambert would have liked Henry to know of his godmother's existence and that she mentioned him nightly in her prayers.

Father Hopkins had lied. There was no such rule about Home boys not receiving individual presents. He pooled only some of the gifts sent by benefactors, but by no means all. Certain presents were far too good for children and these he disposed of through an acquaintance who ran a junk shop in a back street in Brighton. The Father did not know that his contact also helped burglars get rid of articles they did not need. Every now and then Hopkins would go off to Brighton with a suitcase packed with presents, which he deemed unsuitable for children. Toy soldiers glorified war, clockwork motor cars encouraged thoughts of luxury and were banned – Henry's christening mug had fallen under this ban as had a strange gift of four dozen brand new damask table napkins, and a portable gramophone. Slightly soiled Teddy Bears or much used tricycles, which other children had grown out of, were allowed. Mrs Barnes did not question this sorting out of presents and accepted Father Hopkins's view that certain gifts were unsuitable for their boys. So fond was she of the Father that she believed him when he told her he knew of a more appropriate recipient.

The Father's conscience was not disturbed by his supplementing his stipend in this way, while the fence assumed the priest to be a petty thief since Hopkins went to Brighton in mufti; according to the receiver he was the weirdest thief on his list, for he stole such an odd assortment of things. That sonorous voice, those carefully formed sentences, and the confident manner were impressive. Why, the dealer wondered, did this tall, gaunt distinguished man never admit to having stolen this stuff. 'These few things have come my way,' Hopkins would say, or 'My boys are tired of these,' when he opened his heavy suitcase in a back room of the shop. 'What will you give me for them,' he would ask in a commanding tone. 'Everything has its value, I suppose.'

Not all the money raised from these sales was spent by the Father on himself; some of it was used to take favourite boys on Hopkins's 'specials' as they were called, on day trips to London or longer journeys to Dieppe. Hopkins liked going to Dieppe with one or two of his 'specials' because there they all felt freer. The 'specials' made no objection to sharing his room. They enjoyed the pillow fights, which would end in the losing of their pyjamas and starting another game that was more exciting and somehow serious. Hopkins's hands played freely with their little penises and their small behinds. A 'special' did not mind these little intimacies, reciprocating them, or even provoking them. So far no 'special' had complained.

Mrs Barnes innocently approved of the 'special' system and agreed with the Father that some boys, being bright, would benefit from the extra attention he was prepared to give them. She used to say boys not yet old enough to be nominated, 'Now, if you're good and you work hard and pray hard, you may be chosen as one of Hoppie's 'specials'.' She was too convinced of the Father's goodness to wonder why no ugly child was ever chosen; once, when she had ventured to recommend an intelligent boy with glasses and a plate over protruding teeth, Hopkins had brushed aside her suggestion: 'Not pious, Barney. Hasn't got it in him.' The matron was sure that the Father was perfect.

The Rev. Cyril Willindon-Russett, the rector, left the running of the Home to Hopkins and was as ignorant of the destiny of certain gifts to St Nicholas's as he was of the origin of Henry Harlow, of Dr Lambert's act of mercy, of Mrs Lambert's interest. While he was not unkind, the rector found small boys repellent. He was relieved that Father Hopkins was willing to manage St Nicholas's, which he often wished was outside his parish. Though a source of recruits for servers and the choir the orphanage was a nuisance. It was perpetually short of money and appeals, fêtes, jumble sales, whist drives and dances had to be organised to raise funds, funds that were badly needed for the church itself. The rector was not mean: he gave a tenth of his large income for church expenses and the Easter offering to the Home. The sole grandson of a successful brewer, the only son of a businessman who had doubled his father's fortune during the First World War, he had the upbringing of the privileged. Because of an Oxford friendship and because of a distaste for commerce encouraged by his mother, an earl's daughter, he had insisted on going into the Church, thus disappointing his father, who wanted him to take over the family business. His ordination did not eliminate an inherited taste for the best. He got much satisfaction out of his London club; he looked forward to his regular jaunts to Greece and Sicily; he enjoyed the luxury of a chauffeur-driven car; he liked to have a cook capable of producing delectable dishes and a butler to serve them; he only sat down to wineless repasts in other people's houses.

Father Hopkins was genuinely fond of his orphanage. It was so much his. The rector's lack of interested suited his possessive and jealous nature. The boys stayed at the Home from infancy until they left school at fourteen and found work or were clever enough for further education. Some of them returned to families considered suitable to look after them again, others went to live with married sisters, with aunts, but the majority went out into the world as a deckhand or a scullion in the merchant navy or as boy soldiers. Old Home boys who visited Hopkins, would get short shrift. The priest lost interest in former protégés, preferring to concentrate on his 'little family' of the moment.

Henry, at ten, was tall for his age; a pretty boy with dark curly hair, greenish eyes, a straight nose and a well-shaped mouth. He often pondered over the mystery of his birth. One day he asked Mrs Barnes: 'Barney, why haven't I got a real mum and dad like most of the other boys at school?'

Mrs Barnes looked up from her darning, dropped the sock into her lap and drew Henry to her, putting an arm round his slender waist. 'You did have, dear.'

'Where've they gone?' Henry's eyes were full of tears.

'They died, dear. They're in heaven.'

'Both of 'em?'

'You mustn't mind. Father Hopkins and I are here instead of your real mum and dad and we love you as much.'

Henry was pensive for a while, then he asked, 'Does it matter not having a real mum and dad? Does it make me different?'

'Of course it doesn't, dear. Now Henry, go to the cupboard and see what's in the round black tin. Someone told me there were some sweets in it.'

On another day when alone in the vestry with Father Hopkins having helped him change the altar cloth, Henry asked the same question.

'Not on this earth, Henry, But you have the same Father as I have.'

'How's that?'

'The same Father in heaven. God is your Father, just as just as He is mine.'

'The boys in school say – '

'Never mind what they say, Henry. No one can be more real than God. He is present everywhere. Now, come along, fold that lectern cloth carefully.'

*

While Henry longed for earthly parents, James sometimes wished his were in heaven. Rumours about his affair with an American girl in Tours leaked through to Dr and Mrs Lambert. James was ordered to remove himself to Grenoble forthwith. He guessed that a cousin of his, Paul, also a student in Tours, had reported the news in a letter home. Paul, never a close friend of James, had run to him on several occasions: at Lézé's a favourite café with foreign students; at a restaurant James liked because of the *rillette de Tours* that was always on the menu; in the Rue Nationale, the main street. On each occasion James had been in the company of Anne.

Anne, the daughter of wealthy parents, who lived in Evanston, Chicago, had fascinated James from the moment she appeared in the same class at the Institut de Touraine. She was so different from an English girl, so lively and elated and enthusiastic when she chatted with her American companions. Her hair was black and wavy, her nose retroussé, her mouth broke easily into a generous smile; she wore her expensive clothes in a nonchalant manner that was also chic. To James she was charmingly exotic. After a few weeks they had started an affair, which gradually turned into an obsession on both sides. They saw each other every day, wrote to each other every night letters full of loving nonsense. And then James was sent away. Anne agreed to spend a weekend in Paris on his way to Grenoble.

Anne had never submitted to James's natural desire which because of his diffidence and innocence he had contained. Many an evening they had spent huddled together in a field near her pension, up a hill on the other side of the Loire from the main part of the town. In Paris away from her American friends things would be different, James thought. They stayed three days in the same hotel in rooms with a communicating door; each night on their return from dinner and once from Le Boeuf sure le Toit, the night club at the Georges V Hotel, which James sensed had an exciting ambience he could not define, they spent in each other's arms until his self-control was on the point of cracking and he was about to rip her dress apart and tear down her panties (what she wore, he never knew), she would push him away with a strength he did not know she possessed, dash through the open communication door and slide the bolt to. The sound of the bolt going home on the other side of the door haunted him for a long time.

*

James's landlady in Grenoble turned out to be a charming and amusing woman of fifty; she was both sophisticated and mischievous. Her husband, a little, retiring man, who let his ebullient wife run the pension, stayed in the background with their three daughters and son. Madame Bonnier presided at meals with the *pensionnaires*, a mixture of English, American, Dutch and a siren from Czechoslovakia. The last, Lisa, was a Sudeten-Dutch, the daughter of the owner of several department stores. She was older than the other *pensionnaires* and had taken up with a suave American, who came from a banking family.

Madame Bonnier's English was fluent if inaccurate. She would talk in English and then in mid-sentence stop and say with a laugh, '*Il faut parler Français*', and then continue her anecdote in English. She liked to be taken out after dinner for a drink in the bar of the Grand Hotel. The American was usually the host and as well as Madame and Lisa he would invite James along. James took a liking to the bar and the barman, Michel. He would sometimes go to the bar alone and drink gin fizzes and chat to the barman. One evening five fizzes emboldened him to ask Michel where he could find a woman. The barman directed him to a small café bar in a side street. The bar was open and at a table sat a woman. He paused, she beckoned, he entered. She closed the bar and led him to the back of the place where behind a screen there was a large bed.

'*C'est la première fois?*' she asked.

'*Oui.*'

'*Venez, mon petit, déshabillez-vous.*' She undid her scanty *robe de chambre* and lay back on the bed naked. James, also naked except for his socks, hesitated. '*Venez sur moi, chéri.*' She wasn't at all attractive and she wasn't young. She put two fingers on her vagina and exposed the entry, and taking hold of James's organ guided it into her. '*Mais vite,*' she said. In his excitement James ejaculated after two thrusts. '*Très bien,*' said the whore. '*Vous faites bien l'amour.*' James dressed hurriedly, paid her what she asked, which he was sure was too much and guiltily slipped out of the premises as soon as she had opened the door.

*

In the poetry class at the university, James met and befriended Freddie Wills, a fellow Englishman. Freddie, tall, bespectacled, had thin fair hair that flopped over his left eye. Unlike James he was an intellectual, steeped in left-wing literature and a devotee of the British socialist poets; also, he was a virgin. James, more earthy than Freddie, entertained his new friend with accounts of his love affair in Tours and his ten minutes with the prostitute (extended to an hour in the telling) and Freddie intrigued James with his enthusiasm for Auden, Spender, Orwell and the Republican government's cause in Spain.

James tepidly agreed with Freddie, the stronger personality, whom he liked and admired. He was not so keen about joining the International Brigade as Freddie wanted both of them to do.

Not long after James's arrival in Grenoble a letter came from Tours. It began 'Dear - ' instead of 'Darlingest - ' and ended 'with every good wish', in place of 'all my love forever'. Anne claimed that she had truly loved James but no longer did. 'Mom and Pop,' the letter continued, 'are coming to France and we are going on a splendiferous trip all around Europe. We're going back on the *Queen Mary*. I'm thrilled to pieces. Thanks for everything. I was really yours those three months in Tours.'

The break-up of James's first love affair was painful and made him miserable. Freddie provided a cure for James's damaged heart. 'Love affairs,' he said, 'are unspeakably bourgeois and so are universities. We must join the International Brigade. It's the only constructive thing to do. It will take you out of the your morbid state, make you consider real matters for a change.'

James was attracted by the scheme because going to Spain would enable him to write a desperate letter that would 'teach her' and 'alarm her'. He decided to accompany Freddie, whose plans to leave Grenoble were advanced, and he wrote the letter. He also wrote to his parents informing them of his decision to 'fight Fascism'. This was a mistake. In reply came a telegram summoning him home and cutting off his allowance.

'I can't go without any money,' James told his friend.

'Comrades don't need money,' replied Freddie. 'We'll share what I have.'

'How much have you?'

'Five pounds. Enough to get to the International Brigade.'

'Where is it?'

'We'll go to the frontier and ask. The French are on the government's side, unlike some of our fascist Tories at home.'

Filial piety and the fear of being penniless scotched the project as far as James was concerned. 'I'm disappointed in you,' said Freddie, who set of alone but got no farther than the frontier. The might-have-been left-wing hero and the jilted lover returned ignominiously home. As a kind of punishment, James's father dug out a retired female don to give him private lessons in Anglo-Saxon – James was to read English at Cambridge. During the rest of the summer, James scrutinised the letters at every post, but no communication came from Anne, not even a postcard.

*

Henry was reasonably good at his lessons, especially at 'rithmatic', as he and the pupils at the local primary school called the subject. He was not proficient at writing and was frequently reprimanded for his untidy hand; many a time did a ruler smack down on his knuckles. Games were not his forte. He was relieved when rain stopped a football match. He made no close friendships, preferring Barney's company to anyone else's. With Barney – 'dear Barney' – he felt at ease. She always listened to his questions, 'Barney, how can God see us when we can't see him?' 'He's only visible to our souls, Henry. We can feel his presence inside us.' This was difficult to comprehend and so it was pushed into the back of his mind. The other Home boys rarely talked about God, in spite of the fact that they attended church services much more than the average child and every evening Father Hopkins or Mrs Barnes read prayers. Words such as 'trespasses', 'Seraphim', 'Holy Ghost', 'Lamb of God', 'Sabaoth' which they sang or recited passed out of their mouths into the air to remain meaningless.

There was much drudgery at the Home: housework, cleaning work in the church, polishing in both. There were happy times too: picnics on the beach with Barney, choir outings in a charabanc to Battle, to Pevensey Castle, helping with the preparation of the parish fête held on the rectory lawns and in the parish hall, where ladies sometimes had spare cakes to give a boy, or even some ice cream; sitting by Barney's gas fire and listening to her experiences as a nurse in France in 1917, her yarns about her husband's bravery before he was killed in 1918, three days before the Armistice; her time in an army hospital after the war in Hong Kong.

Except for his 'specials', Hopkins remained aloof from the boys. He was out much more than Barney; when indoors he spent a good deal of the time in his study. A flutter came into the heart of any boy, other than a 'special', who knocked on his door. Because of the perpetual gush of praise that Barney poured into the boys' ears, Hopkins was revered and feared. But some of the children, usually those who were not chosen as

'Hoppie's specials' changed their sentiments when they reached pubescence. For then the Father lost his infallibility, yet their fear of him remained, sometimes turning into hate, he had so much power over them.

*

James was beginning to know his father, on the brink, in fact, of breaking through the parental barrier and understanding him as a man. Stephen Lambert was stuck in the Edwardian era; he found most changes that had taken place since that time unpalatable. He could not comprehend the decline in the value of money. He was appalled by the prices at Simpson's in the Strand (an old haunt) and the cost of seats at Drury Lane. No highbrow, he thought highly of *Glamorous Night*, to which he took James, and was struck by the charm and the singing of Mary Ellis and the expertise of Ivor Novello, whom he pronounced as a 'clever chap' when the actor-composer stepped out of his role and conducted the orchestra in one of the numbers. Kay Francis was the doctor's favourite film star; he would chase a film of hers all round the district, seeing it again and again. Over a glass of vintage port he would chat to his son about Lily Elsie, Gertie Miller and Mrs Patrick Cambell. And of horses. He loved going to the races. It was in his blood. His grandfather had engaged J.P. Herring to paint a much-loved mare, but his father had been compelled to sell the family place owing to debts emanating from keeping a stable and betting on his own steeds. The doctor would take James (Mrs Lambert disapproved of racing, thinking it cruel) to Ascot, Goodwood and to less fashionable meetings at Windsor, Salisbury, Newbury, Lewes and Brighton. James enjoyed putting on the five shilling allowed him for each race; he could never, though, get up as much enthusiasm as his father who, when not on the course, would ring up his bookmaker.

The subject of sex only once came up between father and son. This was in January 1939 just before James went to Paris for a week with two Cambridge friends; Gilbert Cooper and Donald Dawson. Gilbert had telephoned the day before their departure to arrange a meeting place in London. Gilbert said, 'Aren't you just dying for a real Parisian bang? I am.' Dr Lambert had listened on the downstairs phone while James was speaking on the upstairs extension. Immediately after the call the doctor summoned his son into his consulting room.

'This fellow who rang you just now, what sort of a chap is he?'

'A Cambridge friend; he's at the same college.'

The doctor's hands were in his pockets jingling coins. 'And this Paris trip, what's it for?'

James avoided his father's blue-eyed, diagnostician's gaze. 'Just to see things. Museums and things.'

'But you've been to Paris before.'

'Paris isn't the sort of place one just goes to once,' James countered, irritably. 'One should visit Paris regularly all one's life.'

'Oh, really? Now, James.' The doctor looked at the brown curtains. 'Now James,' he repeated, 'you will behave in a moral way, won't you?'

'Yes, of course,' James replied, but how convincingly he wasn't sure.

'Promise?'

'Yes,' said James in the tone of a sulky, spoilt child, impatient to end the interrogation. And sons being what they are and sexual desire being stronger than a promise given to a father, James and his friend visited the Sphinx and the Maison de toutes les Nations.

The former in Boulevard Edgar Quinet was the most famous brothel in Paris at the time. It had its own ashtrays (James stole one) that were black and triangular with the Egyptian monument depicted in gold in the bowl and the address and the telephone number round the edge. The three undergraduates were intimidated by the avenue of scantily clothed prostitutes down which they had to pass to get to the tables near the dance floor. The shameless whores shrieked with mirth as they grabbed at the flies of English fledglings.

Gilbert and James chose their partners and went upstairs. Donald, with whom James had been in love at school and who was now reading theology at Selwyn, remained at the table. With an expression of pained indulgence on his pallid scholar's face, like that of a parent pretending to be amused by a children's game, he warded off indecent advances with a benevolent smile of refusal.

James was to remember the painting above the bed longer than the girl with whom he spent a few carnal minutes. The picture was of a lorry bearing down upon a child in a country lane; on the other side of the hedge in a field, a man had a hand up a woman's skirts; on the corner of the lane was a notice which read, '*Attention aux enfants.*'

Giggling, the three friends (Donald accompanied James and Gilbert on these excursions) went up the stairs of 'La Maison de Toutes les

Nations', where, they heard, one could have a woman of any nationality in a room decorated in the style of her country. 'What about a Chinese in a dragon bed?' James suggested just before they met a formidable Madame in a mirrored hall.

'*J'ai quelques marocaines et deux négresses,*' she announced pompously.

'*Chinoises?*' asked James diffidently.

'*Non. Marocaines ou sénégalaises,*' came the firm reply. '*Suivez moi.*'

Gilbert and James settled for a 'marocaine' each but were not sure whether the women had really crossed the Straits of Gibraltar. 'I think they were Spanish,' said James afterwards.

While his friends were copulating, Donald, with his soft, dark hair, chestnut eyes, finely shaped nose, the handsomest of the three, sat in the dimly-lit hall on an imitation Louis XVI chair doing a crossword puzzle, one of the girls appeared and kissed him like a cat. He put his pencil to his lips and looked at her as if he might find the word he was trying to think of on her face.

*

James was anxious to spend the long vacation on the Riviera with Gilbert and Donald, but his parents wished him to stay with them at Droitwich, where they went annually with the hope that the brine baths would alleviate the pain in Mrs Lambert's arthritic hip. Dr Lambert, who had to give up golf because of his heart, was bored at the Worcestershire spa and wanted James there to drive him on motor excursions while his wife was submerged up to the neck in the buoyant salty water.

One morning the doctor drove James to the golf course to keep an appointment with a middle-aged partner arranged by him for his reluctant son, who did not much care for golf and only played the game to please his parent. On parting at the clubhouse the doctor said, 'Keep your eye on the ball, old boy.' He then drove to the Baths, where, for want of something better to do, he swam two lengths of the warm, briny swimming pool. After his swim, he said to the attendant, 'I feel a bit queer. I think I'll lie down for a while.' He lay down and died. James was summoned from the fourteenth hole.

Dr Lambert lying dead in the changing-room on an iron bedstead looked as distinguished and as dignified as he had in life. It was the right moment for him to die. This Edwardian gentleman with his courteous and leisurely ways would have hated the privations of the Second World War and would have found post-war restrictions on the one hand and post-war licence on the other intolerable.

Mrs Lambert bore her bereavement philosophically and saw that it had some advantages. She shocked her cousin, Florence, by confessing this.

'Well, at least I shall be able to go to church when I like and not have to stay home because Stephen wants me to. And there's that poor Henry Harlow. Stephen never wanted to bother about him. Now I can.'

'But Margaret,' returned Florence, a spinster, 'how can you think of doing something you know Stephen would not approved of.'

Margaret retorted, 'Podkins!'. A variation of 'bunkum' that they had used as children.

*

Mrs Lambert wrote to the principle of St Nicholas's suggesting that she might visit the home and see Henry. The Father replied that he had arranged for Henry and two of his other little 'sons' to spend the summer on a farm and if she wrote again in September they could perhaps arrange a meeting. He himself was taking two of the older boys on a little tour of Normandy (there had been some marketable presents recently) and therefore would be away from Eastbourne. 'Henry is a good boy,' the letter went on, 'but I am of the opinion, dear Mrs Lambert, that it would only upset him to meet someone like your good self from outside his present environment. He is settled here and happy. He does not seem to ruminate about his origin. He has come on well in the choir and as a server at the alter. In two years I shall be preparing him for his confirmation, and then, Mrs Lambert, it would be all right for you to see him.'

The world started to turn upside down in September 1939 and visits (Is your journey really necessary?) along the south coast, a military restricted area, were discouraged. The Home was evacuated to Somerset, where, near Taunton, it joined up with a similar establishment. Father Hopkins and Mrs Barnes accompanied their charges and remained with them. The local parish church was pleased to have Hopkins's assistance. The Rev. Cyril Willingdon-Russett ran the Eastbourne parish church single-handed for the duration and regarded doing so combined with fire watching and knitting socks for sailors as his war work. He succeeded in making two and a half pairs in the six years of the war.

James, Gilbert and Donald were allowed to stay on another year at Cambridge in order to take their degrees. Gilbert and James made several visits to London to visit Janine and Colette. These two *filles de joie*, as James liked to call them as they were French, shared an apartment in Dover Street and with them James and Gilbert had a *partie carrée* on several occasions. During one of the sessions the two friends became entangled with each other and enjoyed it, as did the tired tarts who watched instead of performing and still got paid. Donald did not come on these expeditions but he was not averse to hearing about them.

In June 1940 the three friends were called up; Gilbert joined the R.A.F., Donald, who had begun to have doubts about being ordained, the R.A.O.C., and James the infantry. After three fairly light-hearted months in a potential officers' platoon on the Isle of Wight and three nightmarish ones at an Officers' Training Unit on Salisbury Plain, James was commissioned into a regiment stationed at Bognor Regis. During six somewhat unsuccessful weeks as a platoon commander – the colonel caught him in his billet with his feet up in front of a log fire, dosing over *The Times* at three o'clock in the afternoon; he was soon posted to the Middle East, 'Where,' the colonel said, 'you may find time for a siesta, if you're not too busy keeping your mouth shut and your tummy warm.'

*

'Now, Henry,' said Father Hopkins, 'what is your duty towards God?'

Confirmation classes had begun for Henry and two other St Nicholas boys in their temporary Home outside Taunton. Hopkins was now forty-nine and his temples were grey. Henry was thirteen, winsome, and faun-like; his hazel green eyes twinkled when he smiled and the corners of his mouth turned up; he was an attractive child whose gestures and movements possessed a natural grace.

'Now Henry,' repeated the Father, who had appropriated as his study the sitting room of the manager of the Home, who had joined the army. The classes were held after supper when the boys had prepared for bed and were in their pyjamas and dressing gowns.

'My duty towards God,' began Henry hesitantly, 'my duty towards God is to...'

Bernard, one of the three candidates, chirped in, 'Is to believe Him, to fear Him, and to...'

'I didn't ask you, Bernard. Keep quiet!'

Regardless Bernard went on, 'And to love Him with all my heart and with all my soul...'

'Father,' interrupted Derek, the third of the trio.

'Please let Henry or Bernard or whoever is answering finish.'

'I have a question,' insisted Derek.

'Well,' Hopkins sighed, 'what is it?'

'Where is my soul?'

'The spirit inside you. Now go on Henry.'

'I can't remember any more, Father.'

'I can,' boasted Bernard.

'All right, Bernard, you finish it.'

When the boy came to the words 'to keep my body in temperance, soberness and chastity,' he managed to put such sensuality into the words that Father Hopkins looked down and did not invite an interpretation of their meaning or give one himself. He changed the subject and talked of the holy sacraments and the receiving of them. 'Now boys,' he concluded jovially, 'lights out in five minutes, and don't pull a curtain as a signal to the Germans to drop a bomb on us. Off you go! Get out! Scram!'

The boys hurried to the door, Bernard's behind receiving a playful slap.

'Aeow, Father!'

'Aeow, Father!' imitated Hopkins. 'What a horrible sound! Henry, stay behind, will you? There's something I want to talk to you about.'

Bernard and Derek glanced back inquiringly.

'Run along you two. I want to talk to Henry.' The two boys scuttled away. Henry stood by the sofa shivering in his dressing gown. Had Hopkins discovered somehow that he had smoked a cigarette that afternoon in the lavatory at school? 'Don't look so scared, Henry!' Hopkins put an arm round the boy's shoulder. 'Sit down on the sofa and have a chocolate.' The priest unlocked a drawer in his desk and brought out a precious bar of chocolate, which he broke in two; he put the rest of the bar back into the drawer, which he relocked. 'Now, open your mouth and shut your eyes.' He popped a piece of the chocolate into Henry's gaping mouth. 'Now Henry, the other half is yours if you can answer the question: How many sacraments hath Christ ordained in His church?'

'Two only, as generally necessary to salvation, that is to say: Baptism and the Supper of the Lord.'

'Good! Here you are!' Father Hopkins handed over the second piece of chocolate, which the boy took readily.

'I can answer all right when I'm alone,' said the lad. 'I know it all, honest I do, Father. I can learn by heart easy.'

'Honestly, easily,' corrected the priest.

'I get put off when the other boys are here.'

'You shouldn't be so shy, Henry. Not at your age. You're getting to be quite a big boy.' Hopkins took a cigarette from a packet on his desk and lit it.

'Aren't you going to ask me any more questions, Father? I'm sure I can answer 'em now.'

'Them, Henry, *them*.' It was disconcerting, Hopkins reflected, that his wards copied each other's form of speech rather than his. He stood over the boy, who was sitting upright in a best behaviour attitude.

'Them,' repeated the candidate for confirmation.

'It's as easy to say "them" as it is to say "em", I should have thought.' The Father's soutane pressed against Henry's bony knees.

'Them,' said Henry again.

'You can say it, can't you? You wretch! You've got a lazy palate, that's what you've got, and a lot of other lazy things too, I shouldn't wonder.' The priest leant forward and put his hands on Henry's shoulders, blowing a cloud of smoke into the boy's face. The lad smiled bashfully, shaking his head and pretending the smoke bothered him. 'Don't tell me that a puff of smoke upsets you. Don't tell me you've never had a puff of smoke in your face before, or in your mouth.'

Henry blushed.

'There you are! You're blushing. Henry, why are you blushing?'

'I don't know Father.'

'I think I know.' Hopkins put a crooked finger under the boy's chin and pulled his head up, making Henry look at him. 'Like some smoke? Open your mouth then.' The priest drew on his cigarette, leant forward, put his lips on Henry's and blew smoke into the boy's mouth. Henry spluttered and coughed. Hopkins swung round and sat close to the boy and began to tickle him in the ribs. Henry wriggled. 'Oh, Father, don't! You're hurting!'

'Nonsense child!' Hopkins's right hand began to squeeze the boy's knee. 'Ow, ow! No, Father, no.' Henry squirmed and giggled. The tickling began again and in his writhings Henry's dressing-gown came open, his pyjama cord was pulled, his trousers slipped down and soon Father Hopkins had the boy, naked from the waist down, over the knees, the little, round, pert bottom near the priest's face. The slaps were playful and Henry's squeals were not cries of pain. The Father carefully extinguished his half-consumed cigarette in the ash-tray on the table behind the sofa, and then, turning the light body over, deftly took the small, vibrant, erect penis between his thumb and forefinger began to jerk his hand up and down.

'Oo, Father!'

With his free hand, Hopkins opened his cassock, undid his flies, and pushed the boy's fist inside. 'Do to mine what I'm doing to yours,' he commanded.

The boy obeyed.

'Father,' he asked, 'is this adultery?'

*

'I think it was the Médoc we had this morning.'

'Oh Margaret, how can you! It's no longer wine once it has consecrated,' said Florence, whose stay in Mrs Lambert's house had become indefinite now that she had got rid of her London flat and stored her furniture.

They were walking home from the early services. Father Tupper was in enforced retirement, having suffered a stroke after preaching about the impending war for over an hour on Sunday September the Third, 1939. In his sermon, most of it extempore (Miss Reynolds's pen had been busy), he had prophesised that the war would last the lifetime of the youngest member of the congregation, an infant of five, who had repeatedly thrown her prayer book on the floor. He blamed his parishioners for the catastrophe because of their godlessness. 'I can forsee nothing but hellfire in the future,' he cried thumping the pulpit rail, and scowling fiercely.

Mr Dashwood, Tupper's successor, was only medium 'High' and preferred not to be called 'Father'. Ursula Reynolds and Miss Simpson Cox, former members of Tupper's 'inner cabinet', deserted the parish church and bicycled regularly to a very 'High' one in Bournemouth.

'Stephen always preferred claret to Burgundy,' reminisced,' Mrs Lambert.

'I don't think James will be pleased when he finds you've depleted the cellar.'

'I only gave the vicar half the red. He appealed for some. The white wouldn't do, of course. Pity. Red keeps better.'

Mrs Lambert went to the early service every morning to pray for peace. Florence accompanied her on Thursdays and Sundays when the service was at eight o'clock instead of seven. There had been some tension between the two cousins over James's car, a Morris given James by his mother after the doctor's sudden demise in June 1939. Florence had wanted to learn to drive but Mrs Lambert did not wish her son's car to be used while he was away; there was no question of Dr Lambert's green and black Daimler being put back on the road. 'It would be so convenient, Margaret, if I could drive you about,' protested Florence. 'I don't want to be driven about. It's wrong to go for runs in wartime,' was Mrs Lambert's firm reply. The subject was dropped when the supply of petrol was curtailed for private motorists and the Morris was put up on blocks alongside the already wheelless Daimler.

Owing to the premature deaths of Margaret's parents, the two cousins had been brought up together like sisters by Florence's parents and like sisters they often found fault with each other. A constant bone of contention between the two was Henry Harlow.

'I was thinking I might adopt Henry,' said Margaret to her cousin on their way back from church. This was not true and was said mischievously to rile her cousin, who had criticised her for saying she would attend Henry's confirmation. Margaret surprised herself by her statement, a falsehood she would have to put on her list for her next confession. Florence launched into a platitudinous diatribe on the folly of removing such people from their natural spheres, how that doing so only caused misery, harmed rather then helped. 'You know perfectly well that Stephen would not have approved.'

Mrs Lambert said nothing in reply until they had passed into the daffodil-lined drive, then she said, 'Stephen would have come with me to Henry's confirmation.' She stooped and picked a daffodil with a broken stem that was bowing its face to the ground. In her heart, though, she knew that her cousin was right. Stephen would have deprecated such a move. She also knew that Florence's criticism was due to envy, and therefore she was able to forgive it. Margaret knew that Florence envied the fact that she had married (it had been assumed by Florence's mother that Margaret would look after her and that her daughter would marry) and had a son, that she was comfortably off, had an equable temperament, that she possessed a garden that took up much of her time, that she was content to sit reading a book until one in the morning, that she busied herself with good works like reading to blind Miss Foley and running the local branch of the Mothers' Union. More than anything she envied her for her indestructible faith. In spite of her envy Florence was sure she was right about Henry and that Margaret was wrong.

*

'Oh Henry,' Father Hopkins called out when he saw the boy enter the Home on his return from afternoon school with some of the other boys.

'Yes, Father?'

'Look in after supper, will you?'

This had become a regular habit and one with which Henry had complied for over a year; the visit involved a talk about his studies, having a cup of tea, a piece of chocolate, sometimes a cigarette, and once or twice a sip of whisky, and then the 'messing about', as he put it to himself, with the priest. Henry had not objected. Since Hopkins said so, he supposed it was all right and that the Father was, as he maintained, giving him necessary attention for health reasons on account of the 'under-development', from which, according to Hopkins, he was suffering. 'Some boys,' the Father told Henry, 'and you are one of them, need to have this treatment. It does them a power of good. There's nothing to be afraid about it. It's therapeutic. It helps to improve the body. Most necessary in your case.' Henry believed this at first and had even been excited by the visits, but after a while he began to have doubts and started to feel ashamed and guilty. The shame and the guilt prevented him from mentioning 'the treatment' to any of his Home mates. However, when he was nearly fifteen and bodies and sex became subjects of private contemplation rather than of discussion, for being a 'special' he was apart from the others, he decided he no longer wanted to 'mess about' with the Father, who all at once became repellent to him. The thought of the priest's tobacco-smelling breath, his wet mouth, his hairy hands with their dirty fingernails, and his 'thing' disgusted him.

Henry, in pyjamas and cotton dressing gown went down to the priest's study with some schoolbooks just before 'lights out'. After the first few occasions the other boys had accepted that Henry's visits were extra lessons and they did not envy him; they knew he was a 'special' and that was enough for them not to be curious. Henry was the only 'special' at that time; there had not been any 'promotions' for more than a year.

'Come in, Henry,' sang out Father Hopkins cheerfully, in answer to Henry's knock. The father was sitting at his desk in the window, his back to the door. 'Sit down on the sofa, dear boy.'

Henry remained standing.

Father Hopkins turned, rose and approached the boy. Fondly he placed his hands on Henry's shoulders and tried to gaze into the beautiful green eyes, but Henry looked down. The priest pressed the shoulders hard and pushed Henry backwards. The boy resisted.

'I said "sit down",' growled Hopkins between his teeth in a playfully threatening manner.

'Father, there's something I want to say.'

Hopkins, sensing that the boy was serious, released his grip.

'Say then, oh Henry, say! But whatever you want to say you may as well say it sitting down.'

'I'd rather stand, Father.'

'What's all this "Father" business? You know I like "Nippie" when we're alone. Sit down!'

'I think I'd rather say it standing.'

'All right then, what is it?'

'I don't want any more of this messing about any more.'

Hopkins turned white, but he continued to be jocular. '"I won't have any more Mrs Moore"! What do you mean?'

'You know what I mean.' There was a slight menace in the boy's tone, at least the priest felt there to be.

'I don't know what you mean. Please explain yourself, child.'

'I think you do. I mean I don't want to do any more of this therapeutic stuff, messing about with my body, making me touch your person.'

Hopkins flinched. The use of the word "person" as much as the implication of the boy's words making him do so, and the frank gooseberry eyes were devastating.

'You haven't been discussing this with anyone?'

'No, Father.'

Hopkins knitted his eyebrows and gave Henry a stern look, a look on which he had relied to intimidate boys for years. 'Are you sure?'

'Yes, Father.'

Hopkins believed the boy, but naturally he was worried. He changed his manner, becoming the kind friend. 'Now, lets sit down and discuss all this, Henry.'

'I'd rather not, Father.'

Hopkins sat on the sofa and tried to coax the boy but Henry was unyielding and at the end of a flow of cajolery he asked permission to go to the dormitory. Whereupon Father Hopkins lost his temper. 'I've done everything for you,' he ranted. 'right from the beginning. Without me you would never have a chance of going to secondary school. I will not help you if you come in here and insolently announce to the fact that you don't want to study. D'you want to study or not?'

'Yes, Father, I want to study, and I want to go to a secondary school. But I don't want you to mess me about any more.'

The priest adopted sarcasm. 'Mess you about! What do you mean? How could I mess your pathetic, underdeveloped little body about? There's nothing on it to mess about. All I've done is teach you certain physical functions. You should be grateful instead of throwing it in my face as something filthy.'

'I don't feel it's right, Father. It's a sin of the flesh.'

Hopkins rose. He was defeated really, he tried not to show it. 'All right, Henry, go back to your dorm. But if I hear you've been mentioning this to anyone, I'll have you slung out of the Home, back into the gutter whence you came. Remember, Henry, my recommendation counts a lot.'

When Henry had gone, Hopkins walked up and down his study, tapping his forehead with a clenched fist and muttering, 'God! God!' His heart was racing; he was near panic. He thought of his late father who had preached fervently in an East End parish for forty-five years and exclaimed 'God!' again. Then he telephoned an understanding friend and told him what had happened.

It was in a different tone, a dialect almost which Hopkins used to his friend; an eavesdropper would have found it hard to recognise his voice.

'The worst has happened, my dear,' he began, and then imparted the news.

'Oh Lord!'

'It was the one I told you about remember?'

'Henry Harlow? The one who said after the first time, "Is this adultery?"'

'Yes.'

The friend laughed.

'It's no laughing matter.'

'I realise that. Sorry. I was thinking of the adultery question. It always makes me laugh. You must get rid of him, my dear.'

'There is a godmother.'

'Send him to her.'

Father Hopkins wrote to Mrs Lambert suggesting that it was time she got to know Henry, who was not up to a secondary school education and would have to find some occupation soon as his time at the Home was running out.

It was when Mrs Lambert received this letter that she invited Henry to come and stay with her.

*

'Why are only two places laid in the dining-room, Mrs Green?' Mrs Lambert asked. 'I told you my godson was arriving this afternoon and would therefore be here for dinner.'

'Miss Branson said that he'd be eating in the kitchen.' It was after lunch and Mrs Green, the 'daily', was anxious to go home having completed her final task, which was to lay the table for the evening meal.

'No, he will be eating with us, so please lay another place before you go.'

Later, after Mrs Green had gone, Mrs Lambert, about to leave for the station to meet Henry, said to her cousin, 'Henry will be eating with us.'

'Oh, will he?' said Florence, disapprovingly.

'Yes, he is my godson, not a kind of boots.'

'But is it wise, Margaret? Won't you spoil him? And who knows what his table manners will be like?'

Florence was right about Henry's table manners. Mrs Lambert put on her 'talking to children' voice; the words were spoken quietly but firmly. 'Now, Henry, this is your table napkin. You put it on your lap and pick it up when you need to wipe your mouth.'

'At the Home we don't 'ave no table napkins.'

Mrs Lambert hated humiliating her godson by correcting his grammar but she felt she ought to for his own sake. '"We don't have any table napkins" is what you should say. I'm surprised to hear that as I sent three dozen linen damask napkins to the Home as a present some years ago. Now, if you want butter, use the butter knife. This knife. Do not use your knife because you may have cut or spread something with it and therefore it may not be quite clean.'

'At the Home we don't have no – we don't have butter, we have margarine and we wipe our knives on our bread.'

'Yes, but not here, dear. And don't hold your fork so low down in your fist as if you were going to jab someone with it. Hold it like this with your index finger along the top.'

Henry found his first meal with his godmother an ordeal, but she seemed kindly enough and he liked her; he was less sure of his feelings towards the 'other lady', whom Mrs Lambert told him to call Miss Branson. The house was comfortable and warm, much warmer than the Home, and he liked the linen sheets. When his godmother stooped over his bed and kissed him on the forehead, he cringed a little not being used to goodnight kisses – the only kisses he had known were pecks from Mrs Barnes and Father Hopkins's wet-tongued ones, which he had come to loathe – he said, 'What shall I call you?'

'What should you call me?' She was taken aback, not having anticipated the question.

'Yes.'

'Mrs Lambert. Now, goodnight, Henry.' She touched his dark curly hair.

Although Mrs Lambert had had a son and Florence Branson had been a success with her nephews and nieces, both women found it hard to amuse Henry. Mrs Lambert offered James's records to play on the gramophone in the drawing-room, but after the first movement of Beethoven's Emperor Concerto, a favourite of James's, all of whose records were classical, Henry looked bored, and while Florence read *Alice in Wonderland* to him, chuckling over it herself he fidgeted. Out of a bottom drawer Mrs Lambert dug the Victorian game Spillikins, Snakes and Ladders and Happy Families, but none of these caught on with the lad. Florence, having spent her middle years in Kensington, felt she was more in touch with the tastes of the modern young. She, who played bridge, produced a pack of playing cards and fascinated the boy by shuffling them with the skill of a conjuror. She taught him *vingt-et-un*, a game he picked up at once, leaving Mrs Lambert, who had no card sense, behind. What seemed to interest Henry most were the two cars in the double garage: James's Morris and the doctor's old Daimler. Both vehicles were up on blocks. Henry climbed into the Daimler and sat at the wheel for hours pretending to drive. He 'travelled' miles.

'May I call you Auntie?' Henry asked Mrs Lambert, the day before he was due to return to the Home.

For a long moment Mrs Lambert paused, and then, to give herself time to think, said, 'Let's go down the garden and see if any more rhododendrons are out.'

Unwillingly, Henry accompanied his godmother into the garden. It was not one of Mr Rogers's days, and Florence was out, so they had paths, the lawns and the little copse to themselves. While they were looking at the rhododendrons among the trees in the wood, Mrs Lambert debated Henry's pertinent question with herself. She would hate to be called 'auntie', the second syllable was so odious, so common (she despised herself for realising she disliked the title for that reason), and Aunt Margaret would sound familiar and might be misconstrued by acquaintances in the parish. What would James think if he heard Henry use her Christian name, even though prefixed by a honorific? No. She decided that she could neither bear to be called 'aunt' or 'auntie' by her godson.

'Henry,' she said after admiring a dark-red bloom, 'isn't it a lovely one! Henry, I think it would be better if you went on calling me Mrs Lambert, as I suggested when you asked me before.'

'Why? I'd like to call you "auntie".'

'I'd rather you called me Mrs Lambert since we don't know each other very well yet.'

'All right, Mrs Lambert.' His disappointment was manifest. 'Mrs Lambert, have I no proper relatives at all?'

'I really don't know, Henry. Your mother had a sister, I believe, but what's become of her neither I nor anyone else seems to know.'

'It was here in this town that I was born, wasn't it?'

'Yes.'

'So this is my home, this town is my home town.'

31

'Yes, I suppose you may call it that. And Henry, you may always come to this house whenever you like.'

Henry did not take this as a vague invitation. 'Can I really?'

'Yes, you may.'

'Thank you. Thank you, Mrs Lambert.'

'Tell me, Henry, what is the name of those shrubs over there.'

'I don't know,' answered Henry, despondently. 'Mrs Lambert, how can I find my real auntie, my mother's sister?'

'I'll try and make enquiries. But as I said no one seems to know where she is. What are those Henry?'

'I don't know,' replied Henry irritably.

'They're azaleas. They come from Japan. And this tree, Henry, what is this tree's name?'

'I don't know,' said Henry crossly, as if he didn't care.

'Oh Henry! It's a poplar.' On their way back to the house, Mrs Lambert, who loved gardening and gardens, said 'You should learn the names of trees, shrubs and flowers, you know, Henry. Such knowledge will always be useful to you.'

*

'Freddie, do listen to this!' begged James to his old friend, who wasn't interested in a letter from home to James. 'Listen! "Henry –" he's an orphan my mother has taken up in a sort of way – "seems a good enough lad. He's quite nice looking and clean, but his table manners leave much to be desired. I'm surprised at this. I should have thought that Father Hopkins and Mrs Barnes would have taught the boys not to put their elbows on the table, to hold their knives and forks in their fist as if they were daggers almost touching the blade and the prongs. His accent is common, although he only occasionally drops an aitch. I feel very sorry for the poor boy. I was to go to his confirmation but decided not to in the end. Now it's time for him to leave the Home and Father Hopkins has suggested that I might help. He's not going up to a secondary school, Father Hopkins says. I am thinking of arranging for him to go to a training place for merchant seamen. A career at sea seems best for him–"'

Freddie interrupted, 'God! Will the English middle classes – or should I, James, say upper-middle? – ever stop patronising the lower classes...'

James protested, 'I don't think my mother in any way feels superior to...'

'Bollocks! She can't help it.'

'Damn it, Freddie, you don't know her. She's the most benevolent of women.'

'Full of good works. I know. My mother's the same, and my father's a vicar.'

Oxford, Gide, Mann, Orwell and Russia's pact with Germany had only moved Freddie slightly to the right of where he had stood when a student in France. He was no longer a communist but he was a strong Socialist. 'I mean the reference to Henry's table manners, not being up to scratch, his accent being common, that a life at sea would be suitable – below decks, of course.'

'What d'you expect?'

'I know your mother thinks she's helping the boy by inviting him to stay in her lovely home, in fact it's downright cruel.'

'Cruel? How could it be cruel?'

'It's cruel because she keeps up the class barrier between him and her by not treating him as an equal.'

'How do you know she doesn't?' James was becoming annoyed with his friend.

'She may think she is, but she's deceiving herself; she wouldn't mention his inadequacies if she were.'

'What the hell should she do?'

'Give him half her money.'

'What!' James cried in indignation.

'Her income then; half her income. She lives in a large house. She could let rooms.'

'You mean my mother should become a landlady? Anyway, what about me? What about my allowance?'

'You shouldn't have an allowance. You're earning, or rather you're being paid; you've had an education; Henry hasn't; isn't going to, it seems; "not up to it", apparently. When there's a Socialist government there'll be a capital levy, private incomes will be terminated and boys like Henry will be no different from you, and a visit to your home will be a change of air, not a tempting glimpse of how the rich live.'

'You're unfair.'

'Idealistic, yes; unfair, no. I did try and go to Spain, remember?'

'Yes, Freddie, we went through all that years ago –'

'And you didn't come because you were afraid of not having enough money.'

'You didn't get very far, did you? I was practical and you –'

'Idealistic.'

The two pre-war friends, now lieutenants, were sharing a tent at the Infantry Base Depot on the Great Bitter Lake in Egypt. Both were awaiting re-posting after their return from hospital in South Africa, where, by coincidence, they had met again, having been out of touch since their call-up. James had broken a leg after a fall from his motorcycle, which to his shame had occurred east of Cairo, at Qassassin, where he had acted as a liaison officer to a battalion of the Greek Army, made up of escapees from Greece. Freddie, much to James's envy, had been wounded in the shoulder in the Western Desert and subsequently awarded the M.C. Medically both were now in Category B and unfit for active service.

Sex was not a subject that came up between the two often. Freddie appeared uninterested when James had told him about Janine and Colette, and he omitted the foursome episode with Gilbert. Both of them liked an English girl called Clare, whom they had met at a party in Cairo. Freddie called her 'irredeemably bourgeoise', nevertheless he admitted that the dark, petite, pretty young woman was sexy. Clare worked in General Headquarters and to see her meant going to Cairo; however duties being light at the base depot it was not difficult to get leave. They took her out together; to Groppi's, to Shepheard's, to the Gesira Sporting Club. She seemed to enjoy their company and flirting with both of them. Freddie disapproved of these places and wanted to take her to ordinary Egyptian or Greek cafés, but she refused to go to them, claiming them to be beyond the pale. James stole a march on his friend by visiting Cairo when Freddie was on guard duty and taking Clare out.

In the taxi back to the Y.W.C.A after dining and dancing they embraced and kissed deeply, whereupon the driver stopped and cried out in protest.

'It makes him feel like a pimp,' explained Clare. 'We must wait.'

Her knowledge made James wonder.

Clare smuggled James into the hall of the Y.W.C.A,. where, in a corner, they found a sofa, but she prevented him from going as far as his lust was about to lead him and he did not insist. Ten minutes after James had got into his bed at Shepheard's Hotel, there was a tap on his door and in flew the comely, dark-eyed lift boy in his tarboosh and baggy Turkish outfit – an inexplicable impulse had caused James to give the boy a wink when they arrived at his floor. Without a word and with a lascivious glance the boy threw off his clothes and jumped into the bed, and not entirely because he was still a bit drunk and unfulfilled James obeyed the masculine demands made upon him.

The incident disturbed James, not so much because the lad refused to leave the room until the offered pound had been doubled, although he had been scared by the boy's truculence, but for the reason that he had enjoyed the experience. He was no more overcome by a feeling of guilt than he had been in his teens, but much more than at either of his schools did the fear of discovery worry him – he had committed a crime for which he could be cashiered and sent to prison. Would the liftboy tell the management? Was the smirk on the face of the *suffragi* who brought his breakfast one of contempt? He was relieved not to see the boy when he gained the hall by the stairs, and while paying his bill he avoided the clerk's regard. He did not dare stay at Shepheard's again.

'Did you sleep with Clare?' asked Freddie, jealous of his friend.

'No,' James prevaricated, 'not really.'

Freddie did not pursue the question. James did not wish to deceive Freddie about Clare and was relieved when Freddie dropped the subject. The event in the hotel bedroom had been far more exciting, but one he could not possibly relate to Freddie. There was no one in the world he could confide such a secret, except perhaps Gilbert Cooper, who would have understood and been amused, but he did not know where the war had taken Gilbert. James corresponded with Donald Dawson, who was at an army base in Britain, however it was not suitable to mention such an activity in a letter, which might be censored.

*

Father Hopkins was anxious that Henry should leave the Home as soon as possible. This meant stopping him from going to a secondary school. Attendance at the school would prolong his stay and when the war ended, as it looked like doing soon, Henry would be transferred to a school near the old Home in the parish of which the Rev. Cyril Willingdon-Russett was still the rector and had just begun his fourth sock. Hopkins wanted

Henry to leave and go on some merchant navy training course (Mrs Lambert, ignorant of the secondary school possibility, had readily approved of 'a healthy life at sea for the lad') and then join a ship, which would take him to the other side of the world, if not to the bottom of the ocean.

The feeling of guilt that the Father suffered from because of Henry prevented him from selecting a favourite from his new confirmation class, which did contain a very desirable candidate, more desirable even than Henry had been. In Henry the Father had sensed an easy victim, not remotely anticipating trouble. The lad's defiance had been the first he had encountered; never before had any of his boys objected. Usually, after a special had been confirmed, he would either leave or become one of Hopkins's past pupils, and no mention was made by him of the 'therapeutic' treatment; somehow it got pushed back into the victim's subconscious mind and he was none the worse for it. There had been no repercussions till Henry

What was to be done?

Get rid of Henry; that was what had to be done and quickly.

Meanwhile Hopkins had a miserable time suffering agonies of guilt; he did not feel he had done any harm, and though he tried spending hours on his knees he was unable to burke his desire. Lustful thoughts, no longer about Henry, insinuated themselves into his mind. He was incapable of not speculating upon the undiscovered body of Leonard, the boy with the irresistibly blue eyes, the little button nose and the long flaxen locks that slipped over his forehead and repeatedly required putting back into place with an unconsciously graceful gesture of the right hand or a flick of the head; it was beyond the priest's power of control not to recall to his mind when alone the shape of Leonard's lips, the dimples his mouth created when he smiled, the way his left ear stuck out slightly more than his right one, the mole just above his shirt collar on the left side of his neck. With difficulty the Father suppressed an urge to cry out to Leonard in desperation, especially after those yellow strands of hair had been returned to their uncertain home, 'Don't you realise you're beautiful and your beauty tortures me?' It was damnable – 'Whoever looketh on a woman to lust after her hath committed adultery already in his heart' – and beyond reason. He had heard of Roman Catholic priests finding celibacy intolerable; a desire for marriage, though, could be discussed by them without shame; it was a legitimate desire, one that a Protestant priest could fulfil; while his yearning was unmentionable save to a few. 'Christ has given you a heavy cross to bear,' said the Rev Cyril Willingdon-Russett, who was among those few. It annoyed Hopkins that the rector had said 'you' instead of 'we', since Willingdon-Russett was no lover of women; his proclivities, though, did not cause him to break the Napoleonic Code even if they did flout Christian morals. 'It's different in southern Europe,' the rector had once told Hopkins. 'Somehow it seems to matter much less, if at all in Italy or Greece. I get it all over there. You should do the same.' But northern France was as far afield as the Principal of the Home could afford to go; in any case he was not sure that he would be attracted by swarthy Neapolitan or Sicilian urchins.

Being rarely emotionally involved, the Rev Cyril Willingdon-Russett found it easier to control his desires than did Father Hopkins, and not being able to have foreign holidays he gave up practising his besetting sin for the duration. This self-denial was made easier by the fact that he did not find Englishmen attractive: they were too familiar, too unexotic; there was an unassailable barrier between him and them; as there was with women.

When Hopkins made a special journey from Taunton to confess to his superior about Henry Harlow, the rector was full of official disapproval and the contempt of the homosexual for the pederast; nevertheless Willingdon-Russett absolved Hopkins of his sins and as a friend he helped.

Shortly after his return to his old Home in Sussex, Henry was sent on a training course for merchant seamen.

Part II

James was in Athens in a British army administrative post. The Germans had gone and the Communist resistance forces had been scotched. The Greek political scene was bedevilled by the generation-long struggle between royalists and republicans. The majestic Archbishop of Athens, Damaskinos, who greatly impressed Churchill, became Regent until a plebiscite could be held. James was enraptured by the Greeks, admiring their vivacity, their spontaneity, their hospitality and their amorality.

The war in Europe was over. The Greeks were grateful to the Allies, in particular to the British. James, as a British officer felt welcome and at home in Greece. He had not felt so in Egypt, where in reality he had been a member of occupying army; in Greece he belonged to the forces of liberation.

Mrs Lambert's hebdommadal letters had informed James about the events in her little world. She told him about the garden, about Florence, about Mrs Green and about Henry.

The last was at the training establishment, which she had mentioned in an earlier letter, and by joining it he no more belonged to the Home. When he finished the six weeks course he would have nowhere to go, so Mrs Lambert, after consulting James and getting his approval, had told Henry to treat her house as his home and spend his leaves at Gorsebanks when his ship was in port. She had used the term 'headquarters' in her invitation – 'Why don't you make your headquarters here?' she had said, feeling it less committing than 'home'. The smaller spare room was prepared and for the first time in his life Henry had a room of his own to go to when he had time to travel down to Bournemouth.

James was looking forward to meeting Henry, whom he had heard so much about from his mother. He had built up a romantic notion of him as a foundling his parents had saved, a waif brought up in an orphanage and now a sea cadet. He had a picture of him in his mind that was quite inaccurate, imagining him to be a jolly, chestnut-eyed, sunburnt lad with a sailor's hat on the back of his head keeping in place soft, dark quiffs of hair – James's mental portrait of Henry resembled Donald Dawson as a schoolboy. James did not ask his mother for a physical description of her protégé. He was beginning to realise that he was seriously attracted by his own sex and he feared that such a request might arouse her suspicions.

In order to stave off admitting to himself his true nature and to emulate the heterosexual prowess of a brother office, called Bill Clover, James went on a picnic to Cavouri (in 1946 an uninhabited, pine-covered promontory not far from Faleron) with Bill, Bill's latest Greek mistress and the wife of a Greek doctor. After several ouzos, followed by dolmades, keftas, and cold roast chicken washed down with retsina, Bill picked up one of the khaki blankets on which they had been sitting and disappeared with his girlfriend into the undergrowth. James hesitated. He did not find the doctor's wife appealing, but thinking of the questions Bill would ask when they got back to Athens, he stretched out a hand, pulled the Greek woman to her feet (only the hint of a tug was necessary) and with the second army blanket over his arm led her into another part of the undergrowth. It was all very hasty. They only exposed the functional parts of their bodies and before it was quite over, the doctor's wife said, '*Oxi Hgoa*'. An injunction James obeyed.

Although the incident gave James the reputation of being normal, he found it far less exciting than a hurried fumble with a young Greek man in Zappeion Gardens.

*

'Is the 't' silent as in Margot?' asked Henry's instructor, soon after the lad had joined the training depot on the Medway.

'Pardon?'

The instructor, an ex-chief steward (Henry had chosen the catering side of the merchant navy) proceeded to tell Henry about the alleged meeting between Lady Asquith and Jean Harlow. 'Don't you see?' said the instructor, 'Jean Harlow's name was the same as yours, spelt with a 'w' and the 't' in Margot is not pronounced, but the 't' in harlot is, so Lady Asquith suggested to Jean Harlow that Harlow was spelt with a 't' like harlot.'

'Yes, I see,' said Henry, not really understanding.

'What is a harlot then.' Challenged the instructor, who, being basically stupid, enjoyed catching trainees out.

'A harlot, is a..., is a...'

'What your mother was, I expect, you little bastard.' The instructor laughed cruelly. Soon Henry discovered the meaning of the word and he cried. It is all very well being called a bastard by a sadistic instructor if one is not one, but if one is the insult cuts deep. Henry was more unhappy at the training establishment than he had been at the Home, in spite of being spared the advances of another Hopkins. It rankled that his mates all came from proper homes, and although he now had Gorsebanks to mention and he could speak of Mrs Lambert as his auntie saying truthfully that his mother was dead, but his not having a father or any brothers or sisters became more of a lack than ever. He made no close friends at the school and when the course was over he got a job as a seaman in the galley of a cargo ship plying between England and Germany.

*

The war in Europe had been over for nearly six months when James was granted leave. It was five years since he had left England and he was twenty-seven. Henry was eighteen and was to have a weekend off while James was at Gorsebanks. Mrs Lambert was keen to know her son's opinion of her protégé. Henry had given her the impression of being secretive. She had found it hard to extract from him much information about the Home, except for church matters which he was good at describing, or about the training establishment. She hoped that James would bring him out.

Florence had left Gorsebanks and, with Mrs Lambert's aid, had bought a bungalow that was only a quarter of a mile away from her cousin's larger abode. Her disapproval of Henry had not abated. 'Won't James resent Henry?' Florence asked Mrs Lambert, whom she liked to vex on occasions.

'Resent?' What on earth do you mean? James will like him.'

'Won't he be jealous of his ready-made brother?'

'Of course he won't.'

'He'll think that Henry might get away with half his patrimony.'

'How can you say such a thing, Florence? I've left Henry a small legacy. James never thinks about what he may come into.'

'Don't you be too sure of that, Margaret dear. There isn't a son who doesn't speculate about his heritage, nor a ward, nor a protégé either. It's human nature…'

Margaret changed the subject. She did not wish to continue the conversation about Henry, whom during his brief visits Florence had treated as if he were the gardener's son. She would ring up: 'Oh Margaret, now Henry's with you, d'you think he could come round and mow the lawn,' or 'Could Henry go to the shops for me?' And when Henry had finished cutting the grass or returned with Miss Branson's groceries he would be offered tea in a thick white cup and one digestive biscuit in the dark little kitchen. Not once had he been invited to sit down in Florence's sitting room, which she called the drawing room.

*

It was not until some years later that James learnt that Henry had been terrified of him at their first meeting in October 1946; nor was James aware that he had stirred in Henry feelings of envy. James, appearing to Henry as educated, secure and rich, was exactly what the young seaman aspired to be; while in a sort of way would not have minded changing places with Henry, whose existence seemed unfettered by convention and untroubled by fears of disgrace. The job on the cargo ship seemed carefree compared with James's staff appointment in Athens.

James tried to talk to Henry as an equal, but sometimes his attempt to suppress any signs of condescension would sound patronising. 'Oh Henry, do tell us that delicious story about your joining the wrong ship at Gravesend again! It's so amusing.' But all the ex-Home boy would do was blush with shame.

At first sight Henry's appearance had disillusioned James because he had mistakenly imagined he would be that floppy-haired, younger version of Donald Dawson conjured up by his mother's letters. It did not take long for his disappointment to wear off because, at eighteen, Henry was an attractive, tall young man with dark wavy hair, remarkable gooseberry eyes, a playful mouth and elegant hands. The idea of seducing him had for several reasons remained just an idea. In the first place, the boy's being a protégé of Mrs Lambert placed him into a prohibited category of a sort of brother; secondly, James dared not risk a move that might lead to his mother's discovery of his true tastes; thirdly he could not face the embarrassment of a rebuff.

Henry was desirable, but, unobtainable, Henry was a bore. There was little that James could talk to him about. Henry knew nothing about literature, art or music and was uninterested in topics of the day such as Trieste, Greek politics, the Middle East or the new Labour government, and James felt awkward with him, not knowing what to say. In turn, Henry felt he was unwanted when, inevitably, Mrs Lambert and her son, who had not seen each other for five years, lapsed into esoteric talk about relations, friends and the past. As soon as of these family sessions began, Henry would go up to his room and try to read Gibbon's *Decline and Fall...*, a book James had mentioned more than once in conversations with his mother.

There was one subject, which Henry could talk about and that was the service at the local parish church, which all three of them attended on the Sunday morning of his weekend. He remarked on the differences between the Sung Eucharist at the Lamberts' church and that at the Home one.

'The Rector never said the prayer of consecration out loud,' said Henry as they were walking back to Gorsebanks.

'Father Tupper used not to either, but Mr Dashwood has brought us down from the spiky tops.'

'The dizzy heights of Anglo-Catholicism from which precious priests in lawn and lace try to ape Rome, as they wish to mystify rather than guide.'

'Oh James,' said Mrs Lambert, who did not like her son to mock what she considered sacrosanct, and yet in her illogical, feminine way she had provoked James's remarks by the words 'spiky tops.'

'And also,' went on Henry, who had not understood James's sarcasm, 'we had incense every Sunday, not only on feast days, and the priests wore vestments.'

'Not only lawn and lace but brocade as well,' said James.

'Yes,' Henry replied.

James wondered whether Henry's interest in High Church ritual was feigned in order to please his religious old mother, or whether he liked incense and vestments because they were theatrical and camp.

Henry went back to his cargo ship the next day and he was hardly mentioned during the rest of James's leave.

*

While James rarely thought of Henry and when he did it was of that 'dull, common but pretty young man in whom, because of some quirk of circumstance, my mother takes an interest,' Henry, on the contrary, spent much time thinking about James, wishing to be like him, to have what he had. But how? During the weekend at Gorsebanks Mrs Lambert and her son had discussed cars in the garage: the Daimler and the Morris. 'Get rid of the Daimler,' James told his mother, 'it's only fit for a museum, but I want to keep the Morris for when I come out of the army in six months time.'

Henry dreamed of having a car; in fact he had many avaricious dreams, which in a small way began to be realised. He was not slow to learn from his shipmates that coffee in Germany cost four times it's price in England and by smuggling a supply into Hamburg he could make a good profit, and then through the army he was able to get hold of cigarettes, sugar and sometimes whisky which he sold advantageously in London. It was not difficult to learn the ways of the black market. He had no conscience about it being wrong to smuggle; by doing so he was only cheating governments and who minded doing that? Everyone smuggled a bit. Unabashed, he told Mrs Lambert about his deals.

'Oh Henry, that's dishonest.'

'It's not smuggling, it's only private trading, Mrs Lambert. Everyone does it.'

'Still, I don't think you ought to.'

'But I have nothing, Mrs Lambert. I want to get on so I need capital. I don't want to be stuck in a cargo ship all my life. I want to get into business. I have nothing. I must save.'

Mrs Lambert relented. Henry's reference to his impecuniosity, his mention of the significant word 'capital' made her see his point, and at the same time realise that a successful Henry would vindicate her decision, above all in Florence's eyes to become his godmother; her cousin did not despise riches. Mrs Lambert therefore, while not approving of Henry's nefarious way, felt unable to discourage them. Henry had so little chance in life, she could not blame him for trying to better himself. She helped him open an account at the Trustee Savings Bank and she paid in the money herself when Henry brought an envelope tight with notes to Gorsebanks on one of his brief visits. With fascination Mrs Lambert watched the lad's long lean fingers flick through a wad of notes as fast as those of a bank clerk. She did not tell Florence about her godson's black market activities. Mrs Lambert longed for her protégé to prosper, if only because his success would annoy her cousin. She confessed her uncharitable thoughts to Father Dashwood, but she did not put her indirect encouragement of Henry's law breaking on her list of sins; it did not occur to her to do so.

*

To James and Donald Dawson came demobilisation and the need to decide what they were going to do with their lives, whose real beginning had been postponed by six years. The problem of making up their minds about a career was compounded with another, which was to bedevil them both: sex. Donald, like James, had discovered during his twenties that he was homosexual. Neither of the two knew why they had been visited with such tastes – had their mothers been over-indulgent? Had their fathers been weak? The discovery worried Donald, a practising Anglo-Catholic, profoundly. An indiscreet pass at the wrong sort of soldier in a pub had led to his being beaten up and finally made him decide not to take Holy Orders, in spite of a vow to renounce sex.

'I might slip up again,' he told James.

'You'd better get castrated.' James advised Donald. His own feeling now he knew the truth about himself was one of relief. 'Castration is the only thing if you're going to teach.'

'Balls,' said Donald.

'Cut 'em off.'

Henry's ship was taken off the North Sea run and sent on round the Iberian Peninsular, which was unprofitable as far as black-marketing was concerned; however the young man was economical and saved most of his pay. He dreamed of improvement and bought books he hoped would be edifying. His library included *Pears' Encyclopaedia*, Plutarch's *Lives*, Homer's *Odyssey* and Boswell's *Life of Johnson*, which James had praised highly, but apart from the encyclopaedia, over which he poured for hours, he did not get very far with the other volumes. He did not suffer from being the youngest member of the crew by ten years since the middle-aged purser and the chief steward took a kindly, paternal interest in him, protecting him from the foul tongues and the lubricious advances of the deck hands. But protection was not often needed; the ship was small and to make life bearable harmony was essential.

The days Henry spent calling at ports in Portugal and Spain and those days spent by James and Donald at post-war Cambridge were doldrum days, except when Henry's ship was buffeted by furious waves in the Bay of Biscay, and James had his grandfather's half-hunter and £12 odd stolen by a London male-whore. As soon as James and his pick-up had got between the grubby sheets of the narrow divan there came a knock on the door and James's nameless but intimate friend of half-an-hour's standing leapt out of bed, scampered naked across the room and pulled the door ajar. 'Me brother's come 'ome from the sea,' he said with panic in his voice. 'You better look out, 'e don't care for this sort of thing.' James was dressed and running down the bare concrete stairs of the grim tenement block in under five minutes. It was not until he was safely in the tube returning to the West End that he pressed a hand first against his wallet pocket and then against his watch one and found them both empty. Donald was censorious. 'I'm not a bit sorry for you,' he said. 'Serve you right.' So far Donald had not broken his vow. The incident scared James off picking up strange young men for a while and made him decide to seek some overseas appointment.

James and Donald did not enjoy their return to the university. With rationing, austerity, shortages, unsatisfactory accommodation, frustrating means of transport and the absence of old friends, some of whom, like Gilbert, were dead, Cambridge was not the same. Neither 1938 nor 1939 had been glorious years, but in retrospect they seemed less drab than the present.

*

Suddenly there came a change for Henry. The assistant steward fell ill and Henry was promoted to take his place and once his new rank had been confirmed he could not be demoted. For this rule Henry was grateful to the Union, which otherwise he held in contempt, resenting his enforced payments to it. Henry was a staunch Conservative. He admired Churchill, Eden and Lord Halifax; he read and was influenced by the *Daily Express*; he was against nationalism; he was in favour of the freest possible enterprise.

First it was necessary for him to obtain a transfer from his present company to one of the bigger lines, where there would be more scope for his previous clandestine activities. He was tired of the Iberian Peninsular. In the train from London to Bournemouth he exchanged views about life in the merchant navy with a fellow seaman, who advised: 'yew oughter get on one of the *Queens*.' That was in 1948 when James had already been in Teheran for some months working for an oil company, and Donald had begun a teaching career at a public school. Early in 1949 Henry signed off his cargo ship, and after a few weeks at Gorsebanks, during which he paid regular visits to the shipping pool at Southampton, he at last found a job as a bathroom steward on the *Queen Elizabeth*.

New York thrilled him. The lights of Times Square and Broadway, the prosperity, the luxury, impressed him deeply. London, Bournemouth and half-bombed Southampton seemed dingy and old-fashioned in comparison. In America everything was available and everyone seemed rich. The American way of life appealed to Henry. Here, perhaps, there would be no snobs, no class consciousness; here an invented family in England would be accepted; here his accent would merely be English. The main thing to do was to make money and it was not long before he saw how he could do it. Nylon stockings, costume jewellery and silk ties in short supply in England were in abundance in New York. He began by buying a dozen pairs of silk stockings, fifteen ties and twenty brooches and smuggled then ashore without difficulty. Not knowing how to dispose of his contraband and not trusting any of his shipmates, he hired a car in Southampton (he had soon learnt to drive during leaves from his previous ship) and drove down to Bournemouth to use his room at Gorsebanks as a cache. He would arrive about three hours after the ship had docked, sometimes in the afternoon and sometimes quite late in the evening. Mrs Lambert was always welcoming and provided appropriate refreshment –

tea or supper – and after an hour or so Henry would return to his ship, which would be sailing the next day.

Henry was secretive about his doings. Although Mrs Lambert suspected that the suitcase he brought with him contained smuggled goods, not wanting to know she did not force the lock of the cupboard. Once she asked him, quite sternly, 'Henry, what's in that case?'

'Just my stuff. I don't like to leave it on board as it might get pinched.'

But she disbelieved him and he knew she did. He made no objection when she said, 'You are not to use my house for the harbouring of contraband. Next time you come, you must take it away.'

*

It was about time Henry sold his loot. He had several hundred pounds tied up in it. He was able to dispose of some goods through a contact he made in a Southampton pub, but he had accumulated more than the local man could handle, and he needed another outlet. He confided in a fellow steward-smuggler who had been transferred from the *Mary* and whom he saw lugging a heavy suitcase out of a New York shop, which he also patronised. The steward, Cliff Hughes, recommended Victor Barnett and volunteered to take Henry up to the respectable south London suburb where the man resided in a semi-detached villa. Henry and Cliff formed a partnership and they became as thick as smugglers have to become if they are to trust one another.

With five more years experience of life behind him, Cliff became Henry's mentor. Through him Henry was introduced to the homosexual world of the ship steward, that coterie of queens who lead pseudo-glamorous lives on the high seas and rather unhappy ones on land.

Cliff was two people. To the unsuspecting passenger he was a personable, efficient young waiter with thinning dark hair, a pale complexion, a prominent chin, thin lips, well-kept finger nails and a deep voice; to some of his shipmates and much of the time to himself, he was 'Clara'. In crews' bar (known as 'The Pig') the serious, tight-lipped, conscientious steward became (in his own mind at least), the laughing (how he wished his teeth were more regular) alluring (if only he wasn't so hairy) fascinating gay young thing. Off duty he sometimes behaved like a deranged nymphomaniac, flirting outrageously with any 'man' at hand; the men accepted his blatancy, his shamelessness, for his sharp tongue could cut deep and he was capable of punching a castigator very hard on the jaw.

Henry fell under both Cliff's and Clara's spell. From Cliff he learnt the professional tricks of the steward, while 'Clara' taught him the truth about himself: 'You're like me. Admit it. Enjoy it. Find yourself a man.' Henry was shocked by Cliff's bluntness, and alarmed because he realised that Cliff/Clara was right. At first he resisted his friend's outspoken advice – 'Get wise to yourself, if you want to live' – but his defences of objection, of shame, of conscience did not hold out long against the appeal of finding sexual satisfaction in the way Cliff recommended; remembering Father Hopkins and feeling hypocritical about his behaviour towards him, Henry joined the band of 'gay' floating sisters.

Unfortunately, the two young stewards felt no physical attraction for each other; they were too alike. 'Bread and bread make a dull sandwich,' said Cliff. 'We like men.'

This preference for the 'normal' male acted as an extra spur to Henry's determination to make money. To get a man or a manly youth, even at the age of twenty-one, Henry needed to impress.

Cliff provided the answer to the problem. 'Henry, we gotta hit the big time,' he said in the spurious American accent he adopted on occasions. 'We must pool our resources, share the profits. We need a car.'

Cliff could not drive. It was agreed that Henry should take their contraband to the respectable residence of Mr Victor Barnett in the dormitory suburb.

*

Henry had been longing to possess a car ever since he had passed his driving test. Mrs Lambert had not responded to hints about helping her by taking over the Daimler. Now he had to 'invest', as he put it, in a car he was delighted to do so. A pre-war Morris was bought. It was as it happened identical to the one that had been in the garage at Gorsebanks for the duration and which James had sold before he left for Teheran. It gave Henry immense pleasure to own a car just like the one that James used to have.

There was no trouble about getting the stuff on to the ship in New York. The customs officials gave only a cursory glance at the outsides of the suitcases containing stockings, ties, bracelets and brooches that Henry and Cliff hauled up the gangway. Once the goods were on board, the smugglers' difficulties began. It was important that as few people as possible should know about the private export business that was going on between the United States and Britain, therefore the two accomplices could not hide their loot in the cramped stewards' quarters. The bathrooms provided a solution. Henry kept one bathroom locked on the pretext that it was out of order. In the bathroom, behind the washbasin, which Henry unscrewed from the bulkhead, the two young racketeers kept their goods and gradually transferred them to a room that Cliff rented in Southampton. When enough had been accumulated to make a visit to Victor Barnett worthwhile, Henry took it to London in his car. Cliff did not accompany him on these nocturnal trips pleading car sickness.

*

Henry enjoyed the night drive to London up to the moment when he turned into Mr Barnett's avenue; then his heart would sink like that of a traveller returning to an unhappy home. He dreaded the fight he would have to make for a reasonable profit.

'I'll give yer six 'undred fer the lot.' Although it was the dead of night, Barnett in his pyjamas was as sharp as if it was ten in the morning.

'Seven hundred and fifty.' Henry had nerved himself with a gulp of brandy before ringing the Barnett bell. 'The whole lot cost us nearly seven hundred. We can't let it go for less.'

'Seven fifty for that? You're out of yer mind, 'enry 'arlow, or yer a bleeding liar.'

Mr Barnett was right. Henry was exaggerating, but wasn't to ask more than was expected the way to do business?

'Prices are going up all the time in New York. Every trip they're higher.'

'They're not going up 'ere. I'll give you six-fifty. If you won't take that you can drag you bloody stuff elsewhere.' Mr Barnett lit a long cigar and added, 'If you can find anywhere to take it.'

'I know one or two places.'

'At this time of night?'

'Yes. I already phoned someone in Fulham.' At random Henry, whose knowledge of London was slight, chose a district – Mrs Lambert had once mentioned knowing the Bishop of Fulham.

'Go on then, take your stuff there. Get the 'ell out!'

Henry began to close his suitcases. The bluff worked. Henry counted out seven hundred and fifty pounds before stuffing them in his pockets. 'See you in about two weeks.'

'O.K. 'enry.'

The profit on the transaction worked out at just over three hundred pounds, which Henry shared with Cliff.

*

In just over two years Henry's bank balance had risen to nearly two thousand pounds and he had a working capital of eight hundred pounds, a car, a rented studio flat in Southampton, three suits, twelve shirts, five pairs of shoes, fifteen ties and an assortment of tie clips and identity bracelets. His wardrobe and his accessories, apart from his watch, came from New York. Dressed in one of his off-the-peg suits with a button-down shirt collar, and a quiet tie, Henry looked more American than English. He was less fastidious than Cliff, who took an unconscionable time getting ready when there was no hurry, although he was capable of taking off his uniform and putting on a suit with the speed of a quick-change artist. On leisure days Cliff would apply a foundation make-up, pluck an obstinate hair from his neck, comb and recomb his skimpy locks, brush and brush them, and then tease them into position (each quiff had its place) and all this before prinking himself in his latest American suit and changing his mind five times about a tie.

'Henrietta,' he said to his friend. 'I just hate this tie. Can I borrow this?' It was a silk one of brilliant flame, which Henry had never dared to wear.

'Yes, but do hurry, Cliff.' Henry never reciprocated by calling Cliff, Clara. 'I promised Mrs Lambert we'd be there in time for lunch. It will take us an hour to get there.'

They were in Henry's flat, where Cliff did his final preening in Henry's long looking-glass. They both had two days off and Henry had asked Mrs Lambert if he could bring Cliff to stay for the night. It was the first time that he had suggested bringing a shipmate to Gorsebanks. Mrs

Lambert was delighted that Henry, who had seemed such a solitary young man, had found a friend.

When at last Cliff had finished his titivating, they set off for Bournemouth. In their dark-blue suits and red ties they would have passed unnoticed at an afternoon concert at the Winter Garden; a discerning eye, perhaps, would have observed the consciously overshot cuffs, the large golden links centred by a glass ruby and Cliff's mincing gait. Henry's walk did not 'give him away', but the same eye would remark how his long-fingered hands would occasionally flap from a loose wrist.

Outside Lyndhurst Cliff said, 'Stop, Henrietta! Your sister's dying for a gin.'

'We'll be late.'

'I'm sure your godmother's the understanding kind, so rein in your horses at that hostelry over there. The "Vera Lynns" will be on me.'

As usual Henry gave way. In his best American Cliff instructed the barman how to make a dry martini: 'For Chrissakes, with all the G.I.'s you've had over here, surely you've heard of our national drink. And it's your gin we use, too.'

'Cliff, we must go.' Henry was drinking beer.

'Not until I've had Vera's other bosom.'

Henry was embarrassed, but said nothing; he feared his friend's caustic tongue.

In Christchurch, Cliff insisted on stopping for another drink.

'Why don't you call this old dame of yours and tell her we'll be late?' Cliff had talked in his fake American all the way from Lyndhurst and Henry, who was no mimic, couldn't play up to the part his friend was acting. He was becoming increasingly anxious about Mrs Lambert's reaction to Cliff.

'We must go, Cliff,' Henry repeated.

'I'll just have one more and then we'll be off to see your fairy godmother, if she hasn't turned into a witch by now. Being the godmother of a fairy she might easily have done that. I promise not to be surprised if we have toadstools and deadly nightshade for dinner.'

It was a quarter to two. Henry knew Mrs Lambert would be cross, and he knew he smelt of beer. When they got back into the car, he lit a cigarette hoping that the inhaled smoke would mask his breath.

'We're getting near, Cliff. Please remember that Mrs Lambert is –'

'Have no fears, girl, your sister is strictly a lady.'

Henry's heart was thumping and his palms were sweating when they entered the drive of Gorsebanks and drove round to the garage at the back of the house. The double garage was open and Henry went straight into it beside the old Daimler that was still up on bricks.

'Queen Mary's Daimler.' Cliff placed a hand on Henry's knee. 'I always thought you were of royal blood.'

As the two men approached the house, Mrs Lambert came hurrying out through the French windows of the drawing-room.

'We were held up. I'm sorry.' Henry turned to avoid kissing his godmother and said with a hand over his mouth, 'This is my friend Cliff Hughes.'

'How do you do?' Mrs Lambert's eyes did not join her mouth in the slight smile she gave while proffering her hand.

Cliff took her hand in both of his. 'This is a proud moment for me, Mrs Lambert. I've heard so much about you and your lovely home.' Still holding her hand in one of his, he gave a sweep with the other. 'It's beautiful.' Henry frowned. The corners of Mrs Lambert's mouth turned down, as if she had bitten into a rosy apple and found it rotten.

'We'll go straight in to lunch. Mrs Green has been trying to prevent the meal from spoiling for more than an hour.'

'I've brought some butter, some ham, and some beef,' Henry informed his godmother.

'And I've got you a box of candies. I kind of think you like candies, Mrs Lambert.'

There were two bottles of lager on the sideboard, but when Mrs Green had served the steak and kidney pie, Mrs Lambert asked her to bring a jug of water.

'No, no water, thanks. But on the buffet over there I spy a flagon of ale, which, I think, would go very well with this wonderful pie. May I be so bold –'

'You've had enough to drink already.' Mrs Lambert surprised herself as well as the others with her firm utterance.

Henry blushed for Cliff, who gave a petulant shrug and held his tongue. They ate in silence until Cliff suddenly rose and pirouetted round the room saying, 'Now, Mrs Lambert, I want your honest opinion about my suit. It cost me all of a hundred dollars, and it's new! Today's the first time I've worn it. I had to look my very best.' His smile faded when, turning towards Mrs Lambert, he saw her expression of horror and disdain. Yet he went on, though nervously, as if he were on stage and had to finish his speech. 'Don't you admire the way the jacket sweeps down to the vent?' He regarded his reflection in the looking-glass above the sideboard.

'Young man, I'd rather you got on with your meal.'

Cliff obeyed Mrs Lambert's cold command.

Only when he saw his friend juxtaposed to his godmother did Henry realise it had been a mistake to invite him to Gorsebanks.

∗

Mrs Lambert was disgusted and within she seethed. Even to her inexperienced eye there could be no doubt about the nature of this odious man with powder on his nose. The word homosexual had recently entered the vocabulary of the daily press. The local newspaper had prominently reported the trial of a schoolmaster found guilty of committing a sexual offence – gross indecency had been the term – with a young man in the New Forest. Mrs Lambert had been as horrified by the way the two policemen had crept up to the car and shone a torch into it to catch the offenders *in flagrante delicto* as by the crime itself. Both the hunters and the hunted had to her seemed equally vile.

Her thoughts turned to James, now over thirty. He never mentioned women in his letters from Teheran. Like a schoolboy he wrote about things: Persian politics, the wonders of Isfahan, Persian poetry, the influence of China on the pottery and the painting. He never said a word about his feelings for anyone. While Mrs Lambert resembled many mothers with only one son in not cherishing the thought of James giving all his affection to another woman, she was appalled by the hypothesis that came to her now: perhaps in some way James had similar tastes to this monstrous creature seated at her table. Why, when James was last on leave, had he become so absorbed in the graphic account in the evening paper of a man who had enticed schoolboys behind bushes in Boscombe Chine and molested them?

Such thoughts passed through her mind as, with Gladstonian thoroughness, she munched the dainty portions of pie that from time to time she delicately took into her mouth from the end of a silver fork, the handle of which bore the Lambert crest. Her two guests looked down at their empty plates. While masticating she reflected on the fact that this unsavoury young man had aroused in her conjectures about her son; she had not, she began to realise, thought about the influence this creature was having on Henry. She chided herself for this. Was Henry 'one of those people' like his friend? She minded less about him than about James. She had not borne Henry in her womb.

At last, when the bread-and-butter pudding had been consumed in silence, Mrs Lambert rose from the table and led the way into the drawing-room.

Cliff, in an attempt to make amends, exclaimed, 'Oh, Mrs Lambert, what a lovely room! And all these china curios! They must be worth a fortune.'

Mrs Lambert forced herself to respond amiably. 'They were mostly collected by my grandmother,' she said, pulling out the flaps of a small table. She sat in a winged armchair. 'I have added to the collection myself a little,' she continued. 'My son, who is in Persia, seems interested in the pottery there. I hope he brings some back. I have very few Persian pieces.'

Cliff uttered an American 'My!' and went on examining the contents of the room appraisingly, as if he were going to make an offer for them. He seemed genuinely interested. Mrs Lambert relented slightly. Mrs Green came into the room bearing a tray of little cups and a silver coffee pot; she then flustered out to answer a sharp peal on the doorbell. After a moment yaps and a cry of 'Coo-ee' came from the hall.

'Miss Branson,' said Henry, his face deadpan.

'Coo-ee!'

'We're in here,' cried Mrs Lambert, who was trapped in her chair by the table and the coffee things.

The door burst open and in scampered a Cairn terrier followed by Florence.

'You're still having coffee?'

'Henry and his friend were held up,' explained Mrs Lambert. 'Florence, this is Cliff Hughes.'

The dog went rampaging round the room, jumping up at Henry, then at Cliff.

'Down, down, Bogey, down!' The little animal ignored his mistress's command and went on sniffing at Cliff's shoes and then rushing round in a mad circle. Florence adopted a gruff tone (an unconscious imitation of her father, Rear-Admiral Branson), 'Come here at once! Stop that!' She changed to a cajoling note, 'Come along little many! Come to your mother, darling.' Bogey jumped on to Cliff's lap and began to lick his face. Florence's voice became her father's again. 'Stop that at once, Bogey! Stop that or I'm going to church. Bogey, *church*! Churr-ch!' The Cairn slipped on to the floor at the mention of the key word and with his tail between his legs, his ears back, cringed up to Florence, for 'church' meant no 'walkies' and being shut up in the house while mumsy went out, possibly for hours.

Florence made one or two conventional remarks to Cliff, who was smoking a cigarette daintily from a long holder, and to Henry; then after giving the young stewards the same sort of patronising smile that they both had received from first class female passengers, she turned to Mrs Lambert and recounted some of her problems as chairman of a Home for Boys. Since her tale was only about what Miss Swayne, Mrs Peacock and Colonel Bradley had said, Mrs Lambert did not steer her cousin away from this potentially unsuitable subject. After a few minutes, the two young men excused themselves.

'Yes, please go,' said Mrs Lambert. 'What time will you be back? Seven?'

Henry hesitated. Cliff nudged him. 'I think we'll be out for supper, if that's all right.'

'Quite all right, Henry, but don't be late.'

'No, Mrs Lambert.'

'I shall be going to the eight o'clock and the ten tomorrow, Henry. I don't expect you want to go to both, so which would you...?'

'I'll come to the ten.'

'Good. All right, Henry, go along now, but don't be late.'

'We won't.'

'I'm so happy to be here, Mrs Lambert,' Cliff ingratiated. 'To see Henry's home.' He turned to Florence. 'It's been so nice meeting you, Mrs Branson. I hope we meet again.'

∗

Upstairs in the spare room, Clive's imitations of Mrs Lambert's severe 'You've had enough to drink already young man' and his take-off of Florence's asinine 'Bogey-wogey-boo come to your mumsy-wumsy, darling,' made Henry choke with mirth. To mock his godmother was to him a startling irreverence, a making fun of a person whom Henry had never thought of in terms of a joke; it was like ridiculing someone he had taken without question to be infallible and was for that reason doubly funny, perhaps because it seemed wicked, sort of blasphemous. To guy Miss Branson was less amusing because he had never respected her, and even Mrs Lambert, not a bad mimic herself, had done some impersonations of her cousin in front of Henry.

The two young stewards returned from their pub crawl and cruise in the Gardens and along the Undercliff Drive just after one a.m.. The front door of Gorsebanks was open. Henry locked it and the two crept upstairs. Cliff stumbled and said, 'Oh, I broke a heel!' and this set his friend off into fits of giggles. Mrs Lambert appeared on the landing in a lace nightcap and a faded blue dressing gown. Her expression was grim. 'Henry, I asked you not to be late.'

'Sorry, Mrs Lambert.'

'I had to leave the front door open as you had no key.'

'Sorry, Mrs Lambert.'

'Where have you been at this time of night?'

'We went for a walk.'

'A walk?'

'Along the Undercliff. It's a beautiful night and I have so little chance of walking cooped up in that ship all the time.'

'You'd better go to bed at once. Goodnight.'

Henry went upstairs into the spare room and again was reduced to helpless laughter by Cliff with a handkerchief on his head giving another imitation. At Sung Mass the next morning Cliff again gave Henry the giggles by asking at the second ringing of the sacring bell, 'Is that the telephone?' And on the third ring, 'Why don't they answer it? Perhaps it's God and they daren't.'

Lunch at Gorsebanks after the young man's profanity – in spite of Henry's prayer, it had not gone unheard – was a meal of awkward silences broken only by commonplace remarks. Mrs Lambert was unable to hide her disgust and just before the friends left she called Henry aside in the garden and said, 'Never bring that man here again!' She gave Cliff a cold nod in farewell and went through the French windows into the drawing-room.

'There she goes to sit amongst her pretty things,' said Cliff after he had got into Henry's car, 'and to brood over our visit: "Henry brought a frightful friend down for the weekend. They drank and came in at all hours!"'.

*

The smuggling was going well. The comparatively inactive voyage was followed by a feverish shopping expedition in New York; while homeward bound, the partners bought dollars from passengers bound for England – at a better rate than the official one – to use on the next trip. At Southampton they sorted out their contraband which Henry took to Victor Barnett in London.

Henry often imagined a visit to the Home in Eastbourne. He would arrive in his car just as Father Hopkins was coming out of the gates.

'Hello, Father!' he would say opening the door and springing on to the pavement – he would be wearing his dark-blue, lightweight New York suit and his latest tie, a blue one with red spots. Boys' faces would appear at the Home windows and watch the Father shaking hands with the well-dressed, opulent-seeming young man.

'Why, it's Henry! How prosperous you look!'

'Would you care to come out to lunch, Father?'

'There's nothing I'd enjoy more.'

During the meal at the Grand Hotel, Henry would tell the Father about New York and about Gorsebanks. The hospitality would not be given because Henry remembered the priest with any affection, but stemmed from a desire to show the man who had not helped his progress that he had been successful.

However, the visit to the Home did not turn out as Henry had dreamed it. Hopkins was there, confined to his study, and did not see the car. He had aged and did not look well. When Henry told him he had a car, he just said, 'Oh yes.' He seemed preoccupied and not interested in Henry's description of New York, Mrs Lambert and Gorsebanks. The ex-Home boy did not realise that for Hopkins the visit was painful as it aroused feelings of guilt that had remained near the surface. The Father refused Henry's invitation to lunch at the Grand Hotel but surprised Henry by suggesting that he call on the Rector. This Henry did, and was received warmly by the Rev. Cyril Willingdon-Russett.

'Of course I remember you. You were in the choir. Good to see you. You look very smart. Got a car? Made a fortune? Splendid. Stay for lunch.'

The food at the rectory was very palatable, more so than at Gorsebanks, and there was wine. To wait at table was a young, blond manservant, who winked at Henry while Father Cyril was helping himself to vegetables. With his second spoonful of sprouts poised between dish and plate, the Rector flicked his pale blue eyes at Henry, saw the return wink and smiled. When the servant had gone, Father Cyril gave his guest a roguish, conspiratorial look, but made no remark. Over coffee and brandy in the study he told Henry he was worried about Hopkins: 'He's ill, and he won't do anything about it. He gets these spells…' And then outside in the drive while admiring Henry's just-washed and polished ten-year-old car, he said, 'So you know about cars, do you? You must advise me about getting a new one. I'm tired of my old Armstrong Sidly. Thought I might get a Rover. They're good I believe. The fellow who served lunch drives me about. I can't drive. He's my *homme a tout faire*. No other staff. Can't get them these days. Come again, dear boy. I should like to hear more about New York and life on the *Queen Mary* or the *Queen Elizabeth*. I might take a trip on her myself one day.'

*

James came home on leave from Iran every other summer and he would see Henry on the brief visits the young steward made from Southampton; he had not got to know him well, still regarding him as 'that protégé of my mother's.' One afternoon when Mrs Lambert was entertaining Florence and two other old ladies to tea, Henry turned up. James was also there, sipping Earl Grey and eating paper-thin slices of bread and butter bursting with strawberry jam.

'This is my godson,' announced Mrs Lambert. 'He's on the *Queen Elizabeth*; and has an interesting time, don't you, Henry?'

The old ladies cooed. One of them asked, 'Navigation or Engineering.'

'Navigation,' said Henry quickly. A short while ago he had been promoted from the bathrooms to the first-class dining room, not at his request; he would have preferred to stay in his previous job since it had given him time to keep his smuggling accounts in order.

'D'you see many famous people on board?'

'Yes, sometimes. But the really famous or very wealthy – the millionaire class – take most of their meals in the Veranda Grill. They have to pay extra for them there.' This statement revealed that Henry was in Catering, but the old ladies did not seem to notice.

'Extraordinary how the very rich behave!' Mrs Knapp said enviously.

'Funny thing happened on the last trip. I was looking in the window of Austin Reed's shop and a man came up to me – well dressed he was, English – and said, "What d'you fancy?" "What d'you mean?" I said. He said, "I'll buy you anything you like in the shop, if you come to my cabin." Funny, wasn't it?'

James wanted to say, 'And did you go?' Florence said it for him.

'Course not.'

James began to blush; he knew his mother was taking in his reaction to the story and that she fully comprehended the intentions of the well-dressed man.

'What could he have wanted?' asked Mrs Dunbar-Jones.

'Wanted to do you in, I should think,' said obtuse old Mrs Knapp. 'He might have been one of those maniac murderers. Good job you didn't go to his cabin.'

'You get all sorts on a liner like the *Queen Elizabeth*,' said Florence as if she were a regular passenger.

From the story told in his mother's drawing-room at tea, James concluded that Henry was not queer. He reckoned that a homosexual would not tell an audience of respectable old ladies about such an encounter. Beforehand, because of the way Henry fussed about the slightest mark on his jacket or his suede shoes, and his habit of flapping a hand to emphasise a point, James had assumed Henry shared his tastes. 'I'm sure my mother's protégé is queer,' he had told his friends. 'He's very good-looking. I daren't make a pass, though, in case I'm wrong. He might tell my mother. I find him a bore. He only seems interested in cars.' James returned to Teheran that autumn with the feeling that Henry would never be close to him.

On the other hand, Henry had been impressed by James's easy manners, by the conversations between mother and son about books and plays; by the natural way James had mentioned knowing such people as Freddie Willis, the controversial Labour M.P.; a peer who had a splendid country house; a famous playwright; and the 2 ½ litre Riley in which

James was going to motor to Persia. Mrs Lambert's son had such an enviable life.

At the end of the summer Henry had bought the complete works of Shakespeare and Shaw, some of Tchekov's works and a volume of Pope's poems. Of these he had read half of Tchekov's *My Life*, a bit of the 'Essay on Man' and Act One of *The Cherry Orchard*. The book he preferred was one recommended by the headwaiter in the first-class dining room: Dale Carnegie's *How to Make Friends and Influence People*. He found the book most helpful and kept it by him to dip into like Mrs Lambert with her bible.

*

The smuggling continued profitably. Henry embellished his studio with a number of gewgaws: three ultra-realistic plaster heads adorned the mantelpiece: one of Prince ('I've got a horse') Monolulu with his feather crown and toothy grin, another of a Mexican peasant with a cigar clenched between teeth and the third of a wrinkled Red Indian chieftain; two large ashtrays, one advertising Cinzano, the other Haig; a small plastic gin bottle that was really a cigarette lighter, an ice bucket in the shape of a pineapple and a black cigarette box made to resemble a little umbrella – the bottom half fanned out when the handle was pushed downwards to reveal a cigarette in each panel. Henry's proudest possession was a multi-purpose unit, which consisted of a radio and gramophone and cocktail cabinet combined. Above the mantelpiece was a colour print of a galleon in full sail and on the opposite wall over the multi purpose unit a coloured photograph from *Esquire* magazine of a nude girl lying seductively on a tiger-skin rug. The last would have surprised James had he known Henry's true tastes. Henry did not like to pin his flag to the mast and the photograph was for the benefit of certain friends. The bed turned into a sofa and there were two club armchairs.

Although Henry had done many deals with Barnett, he always felt apprehensive when he pulled up outside the semi-detached villa in the suburban avenue. His nervousness evaporated when he was on his way back to Southampton, his pockets full of glorious money.

One Wednesday night after all the stewards had turned up at Henry's flat (sometimes a steward would keep the stuff for himself and it had to be written off) and handed over their goods and been rewarded for doing so,

Henry set off for London. It was a fine June night and the drive went well. He stopped outside the villa, took his two heavy suitcases out of the boot and trod up the path and rang the bell. There was no light on in the front of the house, but that was normal; this time, however, there was no answer to his ring and Victor Barnett usually opened the door in a few seconds. Henry rang again and then, there still being no response, again; in the quiet it seemed to awaken the residents. Perhaps Barnett was asleep. His heart pounding, Henry pressed the bell and at the same time rapped the light metal knocker. At last the door opened but only a crack, no light came on and Henry could only faintly see the pale face and the bald head of the receiver.

'Clear out of it,' said Barnett.

'Why? What's the matter?'

'Get lost.'

'I've brought the stuff. I said I'd come on Wednesday night.'

'Don't want it. Scram!'

'What am I to do with it?'

'Chuck it in the river for all I care. Don't come 'ere anymore either.'

'What am I to do?' pleaded Henry again.

'Beat it! Fuck off!'

The shadowy face of Barnett withdrew into the darkness of the hall, the door shut and then came the sound of bolts being slammed to. Henry lugged the suitcases back to his car, heaved them into the boot and started off disconsolately down the avenue. Before he reached the main road, he noticed in the driving-mirror the lights of a car behind, and then the car was alongside flashing its headlamps and a torch from the window. It was a 2 ½ litre Riley, identical to James's. A police car. Henry accelerated and hurtled into the main road. For a few minutes he gained on his pursuers and he thought, being young, that he had evaded them; he turned right, then left, making his tyres squeal as in a film; he felt both terrified and exhilarated; he smiled to himself when he looked into the mirror and saw no following lights. This little holiday of relief and self-congratulation lasted barely half a minute, soon the headlamps were dazzling through Henry's back window and the police car was level with him again flashing its lights. Henry was forced into the kerb.

'Your licence, please.' The 'please' was sarcastic. The mouth that uttered the word belonged to a dough face with grey eyes. 'I suppose you know you were doing seventy miles an hour in a built-up area?'

'I didn't think it mattered at night,' replied Henry, feebly, handing over his licence.

'Give me the key of the boot.'

Henry hesitated.

'Get out of the car,' the policeman ordered. There were two policemen, one, the driver, wore a helmet, the other, the pale-faced one, a peaked cap.

'I've only got my things.'

'Come on, the key!'

The suitcases were opened.

'These are your *things* are they?' asked the officer holding up a bunch of nylon stockings. 'Get into that car.'

Reluctantly Henry sat in the Riley beside the policeman; the inspector took the wheel of the Morris. At the police station Mrs Lambert's protégé was charged with carrying contraband in his car and he signed a statement admitting the charge. He protested when the next morning they would not let him out of his cell at the station.

'Can you get someone to go surety for you for five hundred pounds?' asked the inspector, his voice loaded with mocking doubt.

'Yes,' answered Henry defiantly – but would Mrs Lambert agree? He was allowed to telephone from the police station. Mrs Lambert's meek and diffident 'Yes, who is speaking' – she hated the telephone – made Henry feel mortified. 'Mrs Lambert, I'm, I'm,' he gave a nervous laugh, 'at a police station in Croydon.'

'Police station? Have you had an accident?' her anxious, kindly tone made his request more difficult.

'No, actually, well, as a matter of fact, I've been arrested.' He gave his laugh again.

'Oh Henry.'

He told her about the smuggling charge to which he was going to plead guilty. 'Mrs Lambert,' he went on, 'can you stand surety for me for five hundred pounds?'

'Five hundred pounds!' Mrs Lambert could not help sounding shocked; although she possessed many thousands, five hundred sounded a great sum to one with a pre-war attitude to the value of money and an innate respect for the sanctity of capital.

'You won't have to pay anything out. Of course I wouldn't break bail. You can trust me, can't you, Mrs Lambert? I hate bothering you but I've no one else to turn to.' The bravado was gone in the last statement. He sounded anguished and desperate.

'I'll get in touch with my solicitor and ask him what can be done.'

*

'Has Henry left the sea, then?' asked Florence.

'Temporarily,' answered Mrs Lambert. 'I think.'

'What is he going to do?'

'He's going into the motor business.'

'I hope, Margaret, that you are not putting up any capital for him to squander.'

'No, I'm not. He hasn't asked me for any capital. He never has.' Mrs Lambert had told her cousin that she had stood surety for him over his smuggling case and paid her lawyer for the work he did in the affair.

'Car dealers are only the old horse dealers in a different guise,' said Florence disparagingly. 'They are just as untrustworthy.'

Henry did not try to return to his ship after he had his fine of £500. The fine would have been more if the police had not offered to come to an agreement: 'Like to reduce the seriousness of the charge?' a policeman at the station had asked him. 'We can do nothing about the car. We can inform you when it's up for sale.' Henry readily concurred. What was it to him if the police took half of the contraband for themselves? He wasn't going to have any of it returned. It gave him great pleasure to buy back his car, to show the police he could afford to do so.

Because of Henry's arrest Cliff signed off the *Queen Elizabeth*. He was afraid of investigations that might lead to more disagreeable brushes with the police. The haste with which he left the ship prevented him from organising the smuggling ashore of over £600 worth of contraband hidden behind the washbasins. Henry was horrified by the waste and emboldened by his recent baptism of fire in the police court rebuked Cliff.

'Why the hell didn't you stay on the Lizzie for one more trip to get that stuff out? And what about me? I was caught, wasn't I? I had to pay the...'

'Whose fucking fault was that? Mine? I didn't drive like a scared, L-plated cunt so slowly to let some bastard cop get you, did I?'

'I drove as fast as I could, Cliff.' His little attack spent, Henry was now on the defensive.

'They must have been on to us for some time, snooping, following us and...'

'Us, no! You, Henry, not me. Or Barnett shat his pants more likely, tipped off the cops to save his bleeding arse. And you, if you'd driven less like a worn-out cunt on a fucking Sunday afternoon, we'd still be in business.'

'You keep on about my driving. God! I tried to shake them off. Anyone would have been caught. Patrol cars are...'

'How often did you change your route to Barnett's?'

'I went the same way most times.'

'Didn't we agree that...'

'It was hard in the dark and there was always so little time. I had to keep to the main road Cliff and...'

Cliff refused to pay half the fine, insisting that Henry was to blame for getting caught. The business association came to an end together with the friendship. Cliff's parting stab on the threshold of the Southampton flat was, 'One can't expect much from a bastard.' Henry slammed the door and threw himself face downwards on the sofa-bed and wept. Cliff, in spite of his coarseness that had embarrassed, his brazenness that had shocked, his callousness that had hurt, was the only friend Henry had ever had. It was Cliff who had taught him the wiles of the merchant seaman; Cliff again, who had revealed to him his true nature, and it was Cliff too, as Clara, who had made him laugh and take himself less seriously. He owed to Cliff his introduction into a sort of fraternity, which, although full of betrayals and recriminations, gave him a feeling of belonging to something; for however beastly they were to one another there remained among them a basic solidarity. Cliff had been the proverbial elder brother, and notwithstanding his insult, his meanness, Henry was still attached to him. He knew he would miss Cliff and regretted the quarrel; he did not run after his ex-friend or find out where he was living; nor did he speak to him, when a few weeks later he saw him in a pub in Southampton.

*

Henry set out on his own to try to make a living out of the second-hand car trade. He bought a car, cleaned it up, advertised it for sale in the local paper, and partly because of his natural aptitude for salesmanship, a talent he did not know he possessed until he tried (Victor Barnett had taught him how to bargain), he usually made a profit of £50 to £70. He needed to expand, to have a garage of his own so he could have several cars for sale at the same time, but he did not like to risk more of his capital in the purchase of a garage. He had no security on which he could borrow from the bank. He dared not ask Mrs Lambert to guarantee him.

'I hope that what you're doing is legal,' she said to Henry on one of his now more frequent visits to Gorsebanks.

'Oh yes, completely, Mrs Lambert.'

The young man tried out his sales talk on his godmother. 'It's no use keeping that old Daimler,' he told her. 'It's just rotting and rusting away. Soon you'll have to pay someone to remove it. Having a thing like that is a liability. It won't even get scrap metal price if you keep it much longer. I'll sell it for you.'

'It was my husband's. He was driving it right up until he had his stroke. How much would it fetch?'

'Not more than a hundred.'

'A hundred pounds? Would it really? Well then…'

Henry sold the old car for a hundred and fifty pounds and gave his godmother a hundred in grubby banknotes.

'We must be business-like Henry. What is your commission?'

'I can't charge you anything Mrs Lambert?'

'What do you usually get?'

'Well – .'

'Would ten pounds be about right?'

'Thank you very much, Mrs Lambert.'

Now that Henry came more often to Gorsebanks, he was anxious to disabuse his godmother of any conceptions she might harbour about him because of Cliff. He pretended to have a girlfriend called Rose.

Rose was the cashier at a restaurant where Henry regularly ate solitary meals; he would chat with her on his way out after paying his bill. She was a fat, jovial blonde, who had seen at least fifty summers; in Henry's description of her to Mrs Lambert she underwent a considerable metamorphosis: Henry took thirty years and forty pounds off her, gave her bright blue eyes, real teeth, a kittenish manner. Mrs Lambert's belief in the existence of Rose gave Henry confidence in himself – was not the ability to convince others one of the most important assets of a businessman?

Henry came to half-believe in Rose as he pictured her to Mrs Lambert, but Tony *was* real and Henry had no difficulty in ascribing to Rose, without knowing it, some of the things his boyfriend did and said. Henry used a device common to some novelists: he changed Tony's sex. When he talked about him to his godmother, Tony became Rose.

At seventeen Tony was Henry's junior by seven years. He worked as a mechanic at the garage to which Henry took his second-hand cars for repairs. Often Henry would watch Tony work and hang around the garage until the boy came off duty. 'I stay on after my meal,' he told Mrs Lambert, 'waiting till closing time, so I can drive her home.' To Tony he would propose drives in the New Forest with visits to various pubs; sometimes they would go to the hotel outside Lyndhurst where Cliff had put on his act at the beginning of that dreadful weekend. The boy was not difficult to seduce. Before allowing Henry to do what he wanted he would say, 'What'll you give me?' He never asked for money but Henry had to promise to buy Tony a gramophone record, a particular kind of shirt, a pair of shoes or to take him to London.

In sex Tony was barely co-operative. He would take off his jacket and shoes and allow Henry to undo his flies, fondle his prick, and pull down his trousers, draw up his shirt and undervest above his nipples, which Henry would gently bite; he would then leave Henry to assuage his desire by himself. Henry did not mind. To have the beautiful Tony in his flat was enough; to see the lad's muscular body lying on his bed, to hear the rough order 'Get on with it!' and then 'That's it!' excited and satisfied him. Henry did not worry about Tony's girlfriend, actually getting a thrill when the boy came to see him after taking her home. Tony would not kiss unless he was a bit tight and Henry did not grudge the two whiskies required to break down his friend's resistance. What Henry enjoyed was winning Tony over; the fact that the boy was normal made the affair more rewarding. Except as friends, Henry did not care for queers, at least not queeny ones.

*

One evening when Henry was hoping that Tony would keep his half-promise and call there was a ring on the bell. The long ring was not like his friend's two, short, jolly tinkles, nevertheless he hurried to the door. His face fell.

'Sorry to disappoint you, ducks,' said Cliff. 'I just dropped by to how my sister was making out.'

'Ssh, for God's sake!' Henry let Cliff in. 'There are other people in the building and...'

'Playing it respectable, are you?'

Henry looked glum. He was not sorry to see his ex-shipmate; he would have preferred his caller to be Tony, whom he did not want Cliff to meet.

'Oh come, Henrietta, you still sore at me? I'm sorry, really I am. I was a beast, the pits. I know it.' He was regarding himself in the mirror and patting his scant locks. 'I'm sorry, sorry, sorry.'

'Have a drink, Cliff?'

'You're expecting someone?'

'Yes I am, as a matter of fact.'

'Prince Charming.'

Henry smiled.

'Well, belle, make it a short one and your sister will toss it back and be gone.'

'Whisky?'

'God! She's forgotten already. No gin, gin on the rocks.'

Henry went over to a chromium drinks' trolley, a recent extravagance of which he was proud. The 'pineapple' ice bucket, several bottles and an array of coloured glasses were kept on it.

'How are you making out?'

'I'm selling cars.'

'How you doing?'

'Could be better. What are you doing, Cliff? I thought you'd left Southampton.'

'I did. I went home to London for a while. Came back the other day.' Cliff changed his voice to the one he used at home, to passengers, to strangers. 'Henry, I need money. Bin' drinkin', playin' the horses, spendin'. There was this guy I was crazy about – oh I won't bore you with all that bloody trash. You're the only one who can help.'

Henry started.

'Remember that stuff on the Lizzie, Henry?'

'Behind the wash-basins?'

'Yeah. You must get it.'

'How? I can't go on board. They'd recognise me.'

'You can get a visitor's pass, saying you're seeing a passenger off.'

'I'd be noticed. Why can't you do it, Cliff? You know where...'

The two sharp tinkles on the bell that interrupted Henry acted like an electric shock.

'Prince Charming,' said Cliff.

'It's Tony. Please nothing about the stuff in front of him, Cliff. And please don't be too camp. He doesn't really know about...'

'Get you, Gertie!'

'Cliff, *please*,' Henry went to the door and let in the young mechanic.

'Pleased to meet you,' said Cliff extending a hand to the sofa.

'Drink, Tony?'

'Thanks.' Tony took Cliff's dangling fingers in his rough hand as if they were bits of crystal from a chandelier, nodded and sat in one of the armchairs. He leant back and then bent forwards and with his fist banged the handle of the umbrella cigarette box on the occasional table by the side. Finding that not one of the panels held a cigarette he sat back again, looking quizzically at Cliff, who was staring at him in an appraising way like a sheikh at a slave market.

'Cigarette?'

'Cigarette?'

Henry and Cliff proffered their packets simultaneously. Tony gave them both a self-conscious smile, hesitated, and then taking a cigarette from Cliff's packet lit if from Henry's lighter, the first to ignite.

'Fair's fair,' said Cliff.

'Pardon?' asked Tony.

'Nothing. You work on the ships?' Cliff glanced at the boy's black finger nails.

'No. Do you?'

'Did. What do you do?'

'Garage mechanic,' he said with some pride. He liked his work.

'I see. Motor trade.'

After a pause Cliff tossed back his gin and then rattled the half-melted ice cubes in the glass. Henry, standing with his back to the gas fire, ignored the signal for another drink.

Cliff rose. 'I'll call round again, Henry. So glad to have met you, Tony.' At the door he whispered to Henry, 'Rather a chicken, dear, be careful. There lies danger.'

*

In the summers when James had his biennial leave from the oil company in Iran he would invite friends to stay at Goresebanks. His mother was seventy-two and becoming more and more incapacitated by arthritis. 'I'm two years above the allotted span,' she would say cheerfully. Mrs Lambert faced death with a philosophical equanimity bestowed upon her by her unshakeable faith. James envied her implicit belief and regretted not being able to emulate it. He went through the motions of being a believer by going to church with his mother. Henry, if he happened to be staying, would accompany them. The protégé was better than the son at pretending to be churchy; it did pass through James's mind that Henry's piety was adopted to please his mother.

Mrs Lambert had told no one, not even James, about Henry's arrest. She had simply said in one of her letters that Henry had left the sea and gone into the car business. James had hardly bothered to digest the information.

Much more important to James than Henry was Donald Dawson. Donald was still his closest friend and confidant. Being a schoolmaster and a bachelor, Donald was free in the summer to stay at Gorsebanks. Although he had studiously kept to his vow of celibacy, he remained tolerant of his friends' sexual misdemeanours and did not, like a teetotaller with a whisky drinker, adopt a sanctimonious attitude. On the contrary it amused him to hear accounts of adventures that happened to his friends and willingly he would go on tours of pubs and clubs with them, tactfully fading away when a new contact had been made.

Other friends of James would visit Gorsebanks – Freddie Wills M.P. was put up on several occasions when giving a lecture in the district; the most frequent visitor was Donald. James found he had less and less in common with his married friends. He was not, though, bored by Freddie, nor would he be at a loss for something to say to him; he still found him entertaining, well-informed and stimulatingly controversial; he no longer felt completely at ease with his old friend; he couldn't relax in his company because he could not confide in him.

Freddie, uxorious and the father of two sons, led a busy politician's life. He had held his seat in 1950 and was set for a parliamentary career, though his extreme views, his erratic declarations and his outspoken articles made it unlikely that he would ever hold office.

'Why on earth don't you get married, James?' Freddie asked his friend in the presence of Mrs Lambert over an after dinner whisky.

'Haven't met anyone I wanted to marry,' James replied truthfully.

'You can't expect to out there, can you? Unless Iran has taken the place of India as the land of hope for desperate spinsters. Perhaps oil company officials are the good catches that Indian civil servants used to be. Better hurry. Oil may be nationalised soon. Ought to be anyway.'

'I think James may marry a Persian princess,' put in Mrs Lambert facetiously, ignoring Freddie's attempt to jump on one of his hobby horses.

'I'd have to become a Muslim first.'

'That might be painful at your age,' said Freddie.

James glanced at his mother, who made no sign that she had caught the innuendo.

'Seriously, though,' Freddie went on, 'don't you think he ought to get married, Mrs Lambert?' It was hard to tell whether Freddie, who hid behind thick, black rimmed spectacles, was smiling or not. His glasses gave him an inscrutable expression that was becoming well-known on television and which made his interviewers and his audience wonder if he had his tongue in his cheek or not. 'A man isn't properly grown up till he has a wife and children. You're shirking your responsibilities as a citizen, James, isn't he Mrs Lambert?'

'I think he's having too good a time travelling all over the place to want responsibilities.'

'At the moment,' James said. 'I've no desire for an anchor.'

✲

'Think! There's six hundred pounds of fucking stuff that's ours, just over there.' Cliff jerked his head in a direction intended to be that of the docks.

Henry sighed. This was the third visitation in so many days and each had cost half a bottle of gin and much anxiety. 'Look, Cliff, I'll lend you some money, if you like, but I will not go on board that bloody ship to get that stuff.'

'Oh, aren't we getting upstage! Aren't we the big business woman!' Clara's voice snapped to Cliff's. 'I want that bleeding stuff. When are you going to get it?'

'Let's ask one of the crew, one of those who used to help us.'

'Let's write to the chairman of the company and request him to assist us. No, you cunt, one of us has got to do it, and it'd better be you.'

'Better be? Why?'

'Because if you don't, I can tell the police about you.'

'What will you say to them?' asked Henry, alarmed.

'You didn't sign off the ship and get your papers, did you? And those cars you buy and sell, you pay no tax on the profits. You're a fucking tax evader. And there's that kid, Tony...'

'What about him?'

'He's against the law too.'

'They don't mind what you do in private.'

'They have to take action if a crime is reported. Better be careful Henry, Henrietta, you might get into trouble with the police.' At the door, Cliff snarled, 'Next time the Lizzie docks, you have a fucking go, see – darling?'

*

Although Donald Dawson detested young females, he liked old ladies and they enjoyed his company. He got on excellently with Mrs Lambert and she was fond of him. The fact that he was genuinely devout pleased her and she cherished a hope that he might bring James back into the church – her surmise that her son only visited churches for sightseeing purposes except when at home was correct. Donald, Mrs Lambert considered, was a thoroughly wholesome friend for James to have – far nicer was he than that godless firebrand Freddie Wills – and she looked forward to the summer and his coming to Gorsebanks.

Accustomed to correcting essays and examination papers Donald had acquired an aptitude for picking out the meat in a composition, and finding in a newspaper article or a letter some bizarre, pertinent or amusing information. This perceptive eye of his would light on something that James or Mrs Lambert had missed in *The Times*, *The Church* or the *Bournemouth Evening Echo*. Donald would read out a fragment of news about an excavation at Susa, which was of interest to James, about a preferment of a cleric in the diocese, whom he thought Mrs Lambert might know.

At sherry time on a damp summer evening in 1952 when both Mrs Lambert and James had finished with the evening paper – Mrs Lambert read little more than the list of those who had died in case it contained the name of a friend – Donald picked it up and after skimming the front page, turned to the inside and read aloud: 'Ex-steward fined. Henry Harlow, unemployed, appeared before the magistrate's court at Southampton yesterday charged with illegally trying to board the *Queen Elizabeth*. Harlow, aged 24, pleaded guilty and was fined £10. In his defence he said that having once worked on the ship he was merely going on board to see friends. He had not realised it was an offence for him, an ex-steward, to go on board his old ship without a pass. The chairman of the magistrates said, 'You pretended to be a member of the crew of the ship you are no longer serving on for reasons that are highly suspicious. You appear to have no job at the moment. My advice to you is to mend your ways and get a proper job.'

'Poor Henry!' sighed Mrs Lambert.

'Poor Henry?' echoed James scornfully.

A car was coming up the drive.

'That must be Henry. Now, James,' said Mrs Lambert in an admonishing tone she had not used to her son for years. 'You are not to goad him. He's never had a chance.'

'That's no reason why he should turn in to a...'

'Never had a mother.'

'He had you as a surrogate mother. I don't think it's the time to be forgiving.'

'It's always the time to be forgiving, isn't it, Donald?'

'I don't think we ought to mention anything about this,' Donald said, flapping the newspaper. 'He must be feeling pretty awful.'

'Poor chap!'

'Poor chap,' James repeated derisively. 'Where is he, anyhow?' James went to the French windows. 'He's wandering about the soggy garden, pretending to take an interest in the dripping plants.'

'He's shy to come in,' said Mrs Lambert. 'He's seen Donald's car and knows you're both here. Go out and call him in, James. I forbid you to say anything about his case.'

*

James obeyed his mother and felt sorry for Henry when he came into the drawing-room. He looked downcast and his hand shook when he sipped his sherry. Conversation with Henry was hard enough under ordinary circumstances, now because of what Donald had read from the newspaper it became doubly difficult. James broke an awkward silence following a few platitudes from Mrs Lambert with, 'How's Southampton?'

'All right,' answered Henry, looking down.

'You have a flat there, don't you?'

'Yes.'

'Is it nice?'

'What, the flat?'

'Yes.'

'It's small, but it's all right.'

'Oh,' said James, and turning to Donald asked him if he knew Southampton.

'Motored through it often enough. That open common at the entrance to the town coming from Winchester is attractive.

Henry blushed, picked up his glass of sherry paused, then emptied it and rose. 'I must go,' he said.

'But why?' asked Mrs Lambert. 'Won't you stay to dinner?'

'Sorry, I can't. I have to meet someone.'

'In Bournemouth?' asked James.

'Yes,' said Henry. He bade Mrs Lambert a polite goodbye, nodded to the other two and made a hasty exit.

'I know why he wouldn't stay to dinner,' said Mrs Lambert, brightly. 'He's brought his girl friend to Bournemouth for the evening. He was going to introduce her to me, but seeing I was not alone he was too shy to do so. I did once suggest that he might bring her to see me. Her name is Rose.'

'He must have left her somewhere while he spied out the land.'

'On the cliffs in the rain.'

'Don't be silly, James. At that hotel at the top of the road, probably.'

'I wonder why he wanted to board the *Queen Elizabeth*,' mused James over the escalope de veau they were having for dinner. 'Some racket obviously.'

'To see friends,' Mrs Lambert was always ready to defend her protégé.

'He could see them on the shore. Donald, why do you think Henry tried to get on the *Queen Elizabeth*?'

'To see old shipmates as your mother says.'

*

'Don't you think that my mother's indulgence towards Henry goes a bit far?'

James and Donald were drinking whisky in the men's only bar of a Bournemouth hotel that had the reputation of being a 'semi-demi', a place whose regular clientele consisted mainly of respectable queers with tweed caps, moustaches and pipes. It was not a bar in which anyone expected to meet the love of his life, but where local 'members' felt free to talk about the loves of their lives, and sometimes gaze concupiscently at a young visitor from the North of the Midlands, who perhaps might like a drink or even a run in the car.

'She's fond of him,' said Donald.

'Not too fond, I hope.' James dropped his voice and said, 'D'you like that one over there at the end of the bar in the green sports jacket?'

'Not that bad at all. A bit young, though. He doesn't look eighteen. A boy. He's got served. He's drinking beer.'

'Let's go and sit over there.'

'So you can see Green-Jacket better?'

'I hate standing in bars.'

They sat at a table against the wall of the lounge bar, which had a dark-red carpet and cream walls decorated here and there with two large mirrors and some photographs of Derby winners; the bar itself was long and curved, lit by strip lighting which made more garish the upturned bottles clasped in chromium fittings.

'If someone stared at me as much as you're staring at Green Jacket, I'd go over and hit him.'

'Nonsense,' said James, at last averting his gaze. 'People like being looked at. They feel flattered. D'you think Henry's queer?'

'He might be!' James went on, 'I wish Green Jacket would look this way – having been in the merchant navy, he might well be. Like ballet dancers or ladies' hairdresser's stewards and waiters are often queer. What do you think?'

'He's a bit swish, perhaps.'

'Exactly. His fussiness over clothes, though, might simply be due to the vanity of youth.'

'A blind?'

James switched his regard from the back of the young man's neck to Donald's pale intellectual face that invariably bore a slightly amused expression as if its owner were enjoying a private joke. 'You may have something there, my dear,' said James. 'He has a sort of native cunning, I think.'

'Forced on him by circumstances.' Donald lit a cigarette and then nudged his friend, who had gone back to his study of the young man in the green sports' coat. 'Look, there he is!'

'Who?'

'Henry.'

'Where.'

'In the doorway?'

Mrs Lambert's protégé was standing on the threshold of the lounge bar, inspecting the customers, obviously in search of someone. He did not seem to notice James's wave.

He went up to the bar and put a hand on Green Jacket's shoulder. The young man turned and his face broke in an affectionate smile. He said something. Henry shook his head and together they left the bar. James half rose and then subsided onto his chair. 'Well!'

What the two friends did not know was that the purpose of Henry's trip from Southampton was to give Tony (Green Jacket) a treat by taking him to Bournemouth, where Tony's sister lived. They had arranged to meet in the hotel lounge bar after they had paid their duty calls. Tony on his sister, Henry on Mrs Lambert.

*

Instead of soft words of sympathy, a volley of stinging abuse had burst from Cliff's foul mouth after Henry's abortive attempt to board the *Queen Elizabeth*. Cliff seemed to think that because of the failure Henry owed him a living. A visit to Henry's flat meant the near emptying of the bottle of gin and a reduction in his ready cash.

'Come on, love, another "Vera Lynn" and then I want ten.'

'I gave you ten pounds the day before yesterday, Cliff.'

'It's my money you're giving me anyway.'

Henry gasped. 'Cliff, how can you say –'

'It's my lolly as much as it's yours. I started you on the game, taught you how to pass the stuff. If it wasn't for me you'd have nothing. And that stuff on the Lizzie you didn't get, you owe me for half of that.'

Exasperated, Henry said, 'Cliff, the money I have now comes from selling cars, from working. Why don't you go back to sea?'

'Stuff that right up your fanny or I'll tell Tony. I'll tell Tony your dirty little secret. Come on, gimme, gimme!' He snapped his fingers and grabbed the two banknotes that Henry reluctantly extracted from his wallet.

Henry was still tortured by his illegitimacy. He had told Cliff the truth about his origin after that memorable though disastrous stay at Gorsebanks. To Tony he had recounted a different story. His mother, he pretended, was Spanish, and both his parents were killed by a bomb in Barcelona in the civil war. The International Red Cross had sent him home to England where was looked after by his father's brother (the Rev Cyril Willingdon-Bennett) and subsequently by his aunt, Mrs Lambert.

Cliff had promised not to tell anyone about Henry's illegitimacy, but since he had signed off the *Queen Elizabeth* and started to drift in Southampton he had begun to tease Henry by threatening to tell Tony. Cliff did not in fact tell Tony, assuming that the boy wouldn't care whether Henry was legitimate of illegitimate. The bastard, however, has his own ideas about people's feelings towards him. Ever since Henry had left the Home he had realised that the only way of overcoming his handicap was to become rich; if you had plenty of money no one bothered about its origin or yours.

*

The second-hand car business was slipping, new cars were less difficult to get than they used to be, and Henry's method of buying a car, advertising it in the local press and then waiting for a phone call was not working as well as it had. He was lucky if he sold one car a week and very lucky if he made more than fifty pounds; often he made only twenty and more than once he had to settle for five. He needed to get more business, but how?

One day Sidney Stone, a local dealer, overheard Henry give his sales' talk to a customer in the garage where Tony worked.

'Now, you know this car is exactly as I advertised it in the paper: "superb condition, as new." Look at that paint-work! Beautiful finish. No rust.' With the tips of his long fingers, Henry lightly stroked the bonnet, which he had polished that morning. 'Have a look and see if there's any rust! Tyres good. Spare fair. Want to hear the engine? Starts first time, see?

Any smoke? See, there isn't any. Engine's perfect. Listen to her purr. Look inside. Upholstery's as if no one had ever sat on it. Mileage? Look at the speedometer. Only done twelve thousand. Yes, it's three years old. Twelve thousand in three years is nothing, that's what a car does in one year normally, so you're buying yourself a one-year-old car and a one-owner car for the price of a three-year-old car. It's a bargain; there's no other word for it. I must have been crazy to only have put £474 in the paper, but I'm sticking to that price. I should have asked for at least a hundred more. With a new car you drop at least two hundred as soon as you drive it out of the garage. That's not so with this one. You could sell it for more than you gave for it after a year's hard use...'

Mr Stone sat in his Jaguar listening to this performance. He was impressed. He needed a salesman and Henry, neatly turned out, clean looking, young with just the sort of persuasive manner required, seemed the right person. He waited until Henry had come back from a trial run with the prospective purchases, whose offer of £425 was accepted and the called the young salesman over.

'How much did you make on that deal?' he asked.

'I bought it last week for £300,' lied Henry, 'and spent an hour's elbow grease on it.'

'Like to come to my place for a chat?' asked Mr Stone. 'I've an idea we might do business together.'

In his old Morris Henry had difficulty in keeping up with Stone, who, in his new Jaguar, ignored the speed limit. Stone's house concealed by trees and shrubs was off the Winchester road at the end of the common. The outside of the house was in the style of the 1930s with gables and red brick. The spacious lounge was Henry's idea of what a sitting-room should be: far more wonderful than Mrs Lamberts drawing-room, which was horribly old fashioned in comparison, the room boasted a huge television set-record-player-radio-tape recorder complex, a cocktail bar with chromium fittings, armchairs, made, it seemed for two or persons of great bulk, a massive sofa smothered with cushions of many colours, a fitted carpet, dark-blue with a pile one's feet sank into like that in the foyer of a new cinema, two chandeliers, gaudy Chinese vases converted into lamps, glass-covered occasional tables on which were red and black ashtrays the size of dishes, and abstract paintings that screamed their presence from the walls. Henry wasn't sure about the pictures but apart from them he thought it was the most magnificent room he had ever seen.

'Fine place you've got here,' he said, remembering the line from a film.

'Like it?'

'You bet.'

It was almost as it they were in the film.

'Drink?' Bald and stout, Sidney Stone pulled up the flap of the bar and squeezed through to the other side. He switched on a garland of fairy lights and at the same time a sign in red which said, 'Sid's Bar.'

Henry gulped. 'Highball, please.'

Mr Stone poured out a whisky and soda, fished two ice cubes from an ice bucked with two hairy fingers (a third finger bore a diamond solitaire), plopped the ice cubes into the glass, stirred the contents with a swizzlestick and pushed the concoction towards Henry, now perched on a bar stool.

'Cigar?'

'No thanks.'

'Come on.'

'Thanks.'

Henry did not much care for cigars; however he had smoked them in his *Queen Elizabeth* days and was able to do so unselfconsciously. Mr Stone poured himself a Coca-Cola, struggled out from behind Sid's Bar and with his podgy fingers extended indicated one of the capacious lounge chairs. 'I've brought you here to talk business,' he said.

'So you said, but you don't want a car, do you?'

Stone laughed in the way a managing director laughs at a junior employee's sycophantic joke. 'I'm a dealer like you, in a rather bigger way actually. I was impressed by your manner when you were selling that old Rover, thought maybe we could do something together. Now, my idea is this...'

It sounded simple. He wanted Henry to be a salesman on a commission basis. 'I supply the cars, you sell them. I want you to be in charge of my showroom. You know it, don't you? The man I've got there now hasn't enough drive. I'm sacking him and I'd like you to take over. I'll give you fifty percent commission on every car you sell. And my cars are quality. What d'you say?'

'I'll have to think about it.' After his experience with Cliff and Victor Barnett, the idea of working for anyone, even though the terms seemed reasonable, did not greatly appeal to him.

Sidney Stone pulled the cigar from his mouth and through a cloud of expensive smoke, snapped, 'How much you make a week?'

'About a hundred and fifty,' Henry lied. 'Sometimes more.'

'How many cars you sell a week?'

'Three, four.' Henry had never sold more than two. The luxurious room, Sidney's strong highball and the aroma of the cigars prompted him to exaggerate. He wondered if his host believed him.

'Average profit on a car?'

'Fifty.'

'Sensible. Quick turnover, quick profit.'

'That's what I say.' Henry smiled. He had often used the cliché to himself.

'In charge of that showroom you should make about two-fifty a week. I'd leave the pricing to you and the advertising. The higher you sell for the more for you.'

A woman with daffodil-yellow hair came into the room. 'My wife, Daphne,' Sidney said, gravely, as if presenting an angel, Henry thought. She was wearing a plain black dress and her hands were liberally ringed, a diamond brooch glistened from her left breast and round her neck was a pearl necklace matched by pearl earrings. Henry felt he had entered the world of his own make-believe: Daphne resembled the Rose of his fantasy.

'Pleased to meet you, Mrs Stone.' Henry had learnt from Dale Carnegie's book that the sweetest sound to a person was his own name. He had pondered over this instruction and decided that the great Carnegie was not always right since he hated people saying Harlow; he came to the conclusion that his case must be exceptional and he obeyed his favourite author's advice when he met someone for the first time.

With a grunt Sidney got out of his chair and went behind the bar and while he was mixing his wife a dry martini Henry glanced at Daphne, who like an exotic feline had settled among the cushions and then with greater admiration at the giant television set – 'If only I had a place like this to invite Tony to,' he mused to himself.

The three dragged through a sludge of small talk about the weather and Southampton before Daphne asked the question for which Henry steeled himself whenever he met someone new. 'You were born here?'

'No, Mrs Stone, in Bournemouth.' Henry did not always use the Spanish story; it depended on whom he was meeting.

'Your parents are in Bournemouth?'

'A wealthy town,' put in Sidney.

'My parents passed away.'

'I'm sorry,' Daphne looked down at her bejewelled hand which was stroking sensually a pink cushion.

'My aunt lives in Bournemouth, Mrs Stone. She's my godmother too.'

'That's nice,' said Daphne.

'Why didn't you set up business in Bournemouth?' asked Sidney. 'There's more money there than here.'

'Bournemouth's stagnant; here's growing.'

Sidney nodded.

Encouraged, Henry continued, 'In Bournemouth people buy new cars mostly. Here there's a working class that's earning more and more and they go for second-hand cars; they can't afford new ones.'

'True.'

The cigar and the highball had helped Henry inflate himself into the big business man. 'Also,' he added, 'I have contracts with the shipping people.'

'Oh, do you?' said Sidney, interested.

Henry promised to let the apparently wealthy Sidney Stone know his decision about the offered job in a few days, and after accepting another highball, which he drank to the accompaniment of soft background music put on by Daphne, he rose to leave. In the hall, Sidney turned a switch and the rise of each stair became illuminated with coloured lights. 'I call it the rainbow staircase,' he said. 'Like it?' he asked, as if it were for sale.

'Wonderful!' sighed Henry. Then he added, forgetting it was a song title, 'Stairway to the stars.'

Sid Stone chuckled. 'That's good that is, Henry. Me and you are getting along.'

*

Mrs Lambert was pleased when Henry told her he had entered into a business partnership with the 'fabulously rich' Sidney Stone and that he had a secure job. Her godson came to see her now and then and would tell her about the Stones, who sounded materialistic and vulgar, not at all the sort of people she fancied meeting; she listened patiently to Henry's description of the Stones' mansion. 'If only I could have a house like that,' said Henry to Mrs Lambert.

'I expect you will one day.'

'Do you really? How could I, though, Mrs Lambert?'

'People do make fortunes. I don't see why you shouldn't make one.'

Henry was delighted. He told his godmother about Mrs Stone, describing her beauty and her 'fabulous' jewellery. 'She always wears diamonds, pearls and rubies.'

'At the same time?'

Mrs Lambert laughed to herself at such a bedizening.

'She's like a goddess.'

'And what about Rose?'

'I'd like to give her diamonds and pearls and rubies too.'

In her weekly letter to James, Mrs Lambert told him about Henry's new friends. 'They sound flashy,' she wrote, and expressed the hope that they were not mixed up in anything shady. 'There do seem to be great possibilities in the car trade, according to Henry, who now speaks in terms of hundreds when he talks of money. One can't blame the poor boy for trying to pull himself up. He talks much of his girlfriend Rose. I wonder if it will come to anything. I think it would be a blessing if Henry got married. If he did, he would have real relations; also, marriage would give him responsibility, which he needs; it would make him steadier. After all, many would say it was high time he found a wife.'

James read in this letter a hint that his mother would like him to find a wife. He had no intention of doing so; nevertheless he was anxious that his mother should be unaware of his predilection; he was not sure that she was. How enviable the lives of married people seemed! They would call the mere breaking of a plate a calamity, while to him real disaster in the form of robbery, arrest, a beating-up, a demand for money at the point of a knife were ever present. What a joy it must be, James thought, to lead an open existence and not have to divide one's life into separate compartments.

*

Cliff was becoming more and more obnoxious. He kept calling at Henry's flat and if he was not given what he asked for (several gins and money) he would resort to menaces. A new threat was added to the old ones about telling Tony of Henry's illegitimacy and the Inland Revenue about tax evasion.

'You're working for that swollen slob Sid Stone, aren't you?'

'How d'you know?'

'Sid isn't just selling cars, is he?'

'That's all I know he does,' replied Henry, truthfully, although three months of working for Stone made him wonder where the cars came from. After one had been sold, he obeyed instructions by telephoning a London number and the next day another would appear that quite lived up to his habitual advertisement tag: 'as new'. Sid, who was often unavailable, advised him to ask a price below the list one.

'An old boiling fowl told me that Stone's cars are pinched.'

'Who told you that?'

'Never mind. It may not be true but it's a red hot rumour that I could send flashing round this flaming town. You'd be in for it as an accomplice.'

'How much?' asked Henry.

'How quick on the ball my sister has become since she entered big business. Fifty, please.'

'*Fifty?*'

'Yeah, that'll do for the moment, ducks.'

'Haven't got it here.'

'Stuff that, Henry, right up. Gimme!'

'I don't have any money here, Cliff, look!' Henry whipped out his wallet and showed him the two pound notes it contained. I never keep any money here. I keep in the Savings Bank.'

'Don't kid me.' Cliff rose. He was unsteady on his feet and the whites of his eyes were the colour of a boiled lobster.

'It's true, Cliff. If I had it here, I'd give it to you, though fifty is a hell of a lot.'

'You've got your fucking lolly here somewhere.' Cliff plunged across to a small bookcase next the cocktail cabinet and pulled out from the half-empty bookshelves one by one the unread volumes, dropping them on the floor after he had clumsily flicked through the pages. The crimson vase containing artificial daffodils on top of the bookcase wobbled dangerously.

'You can search the whole place. You won't find any money, 'cause I don't keep cash around.'

Cliff let fall Boswell's *Life of Johnson*. 'I suppose that bloody crook you work for...' he broke off; his train of thought lost in his fuddled mind.

'I'll let you have some money tomorrow, Cliff.'

'Fifty, I need it. All right, ducks.' At the door he said, 'Sorry forgot to ask, how's the boyfriend?'

'Called up.'

'Oh dear, how unkind of His, I mean Her Majesty. See you tomorrow, Maud. Same time?'

'Yes, seven.'

As soon as Henry had closed the door, he let out a sigh of relief; then, sweating, he hurried over to the bookcase, grasped the vase, removed the daffodils, plunged his hand inside and drew out two wads of banknotes. 'Thank God he was drunk!' he exclaimed. Breathing hard he counted his hoard as if Cliff might have spirited some of the notes away. He then stuffed the money into his brief case and peeping through a chink in the curtains he made sure that Cliff was not lurking in the street. He rang Sidney Stone, who didn't like to be visited without a previous arrangement and in any case was often away. By chance he was in and answered the phone.

'I must come and see you,' said Henry.

'Its not convenient now,' replied the dealer.

'It's urgent. I must see you.'

'What about? Something gone wrong?'

'Yes and it concerns you.'

'Can't it wait until tomorrow?'

'No.'

'All right, come along then.'

*

When Henry had told Sidney Stone what his ex-shipmate had said, the dealer did not seem unduly concerned. Across the bar he said to Henry, 'We'll fix him.'

'It's not true, is it?' asked Henry accepting a highball.

'What?'

'That the cars I get are stolen?'

'Course they bloody are. What did you think?'

Henry's hand shook as he raised his freezing glass to his lips.

'Don't get scared!' commanded Sid in his unpleasant hoarse voice. 'There's not a chance in a thousand of us being found out. No one can prove anything. Those I get lifted from the south get sent to the Midlands or the North and the other way round. At my London place we cannibalise: changing back axles, engines, even driving shafts, and of course we re-spray. You're only one of our sellers. You're doing fine. Don't shit your pants over this, Henry. Let Sid fix it. Sid can fix most things. Now tomorrow evening at ... what time is it that this charming pal of yours is coming round?'

'Seven.'

'Tomorrow at seven we'll play it like this: first you...

*

In the fifties Muhammad Moussadeq became prime minister of Iran. He nationalised the foreign oil company in the Gulf, thereby pleasing one Englishman at least: Freddie Wills M.P. Freddie had often spoken of the illogicality of Britain nationalising her own resources and complaining when other countries nationalised theirs. 'We are no longer an imperial power, thank God!' he would declare. 'We must base our foreign relations, not on the exploitation of skinny dark people, who've never had a square meal in their lives, not on the threat of force, not on empty promises disguised by mealy-mouthed diplomats to look like good intentions, but on fair and honest commercial agreements that benefit both parties equally. When I hear that a country has nationalised its mines, its oil fields, its plantations, its means of transport, its power stations or telephone companies, which hitherto had kept British capitalists in idle comfort, I say "Bloody good show!"'

James's job in Iran came to an end and he was transferred to an enclave of oil administrators and engineers and their wives in Northern Iraq. He found the stratified class system of graded employees and the insularity of the compound with its graded concrete blocks containing people with identical furniture, food and outlook and almost identical photographs of mothers and children in the U.K., so unbearable, so incompatible with his philosophy (contact with the 'locals' outside working hours was discouraged) that after a year's confinement he resigned, turning into cash a generous provident fund.

He planned to motor slowly home and he left Iraq with that intention. By the time he reached Beirut a feeling of such despondency came over him, caused by contemplation during hours at the driving wheel of the dangers of both the meteorological and the social of climate of England, that he went no farther. He informed his mother that he had decided to spend the winter (it was September), in Lebanon trying to write a book. Mrs Lambert warmly approved of her son's decision. 'It's much better,' she wrote, 'for you to be there where you are, free to do as you please, than in this land of restrictions and limitations.' What did she mean? Was she referring to the unavoidable curbing of individual freedom that a 'fair shares for all' policy was bound to bring about eventually? Or did she suspect that James might get into trouble if he lived in England? Had his continued lack of interest in girls finally convinced her of the truth?

*

'Florence, I've been remaking my will.' Mrs Lambert often brought up the subject of her will when she wanted to retaliate to a sting from her cousin. Two days before, Florence had said in her father's voice, which was tinged with peevishness: 'I can't think why you go on living in this house. It's much too big for you to manage with the garden as well. You should move into a flat. They are converting the Gables into service flats and Mrs Knapp says...'

'I've no intention of moving into a flat. What would James and Henry do with nowhere to go when they came home?'

'They're hardly ever here, Margaret dear. Henry can come over for the day from Southampton easily enough, and James, well, he could afford a hotel, or I could put him up.'

Roused by the last suggestion, Mrs Lambert said, firmly, 'I like this house. I shall die in it. Too big it may be, but it's James's home and it's Henry's home.' She had never regarded it exactly as Henry's home; she called it so to irritate her cousin.

'With your becoming more incapacitated with your arthritis – one must face facts – you'd be happier on one floor.'

'Florence, I've just said and I mean it, I have not the slightest intention of leaving this house. Now that Miss Phillips is here to help...'

'Miss Phillips!' Florence exclaimed in a mocking tone. She disliked Mrs Lambert's companion, a recent acquisition insisted upon by James.

'What good is she? Why, only last week you were struggling upstairs with trays of food for her.'

'She was ill.'

'Ill!'

Although Mrs Lambert could never be accused of harbouring vengeance, she was capable of a mild reprisal. This she delivered two days later beginning with the statement about the redrafting of her will.

'You're always changing your will,' sneered Florence, who having much less to leave than Margaret, did not enjoy hearing about her cousin's proposed bequests.

'Making or remaking a will one of the few amusements left in old age.'

'Only when one has a lot to leave.'

'Now,' began Mrs Lambert, childishly eager to impart her plans, 'in my previous will I left two thousand to the National Trust, one to Henry's Home, one to the U.M.C.A., one to the Mission to Seamen – they do such good work providing people like Henry with a decent place to go to in foreign parts. I've decided to raise all the amounts by five hundred. What do you think?'

'I should reduce them by five hundred. As I've said before Margaret, it's one relatives one should look after first.'

'If no one thought about charities, all the organisations that do good works would have to close down.'

'In these days of social security, whatever they call it, charities are less and less necessary.'

'It'll be a sad day, Florence, when, if one wants to help good causes one'll have to leave money specifically to the Chancellor of the Exchequer – as if he didn't extort enough from one's estate already. Oh dear, isn't it a pity one won't be alive when one's will is read. I'd love to see the expression on some people's faces.'

'What about Henry?' asked Florence. 'What will you leave him?' She would have liked to substitute herself for Henry, but she could not bring herself to ask Margaret outright what she was going to leave her. She had thought of suggesting a pact whereby they would agree to leave each other the same amount, but had qualms in doing so.

'I was going ask you that, Florence. What do you think, five or ten thousand?

'You know what I think, Margaret. We've been through all that before.'

'I shall leave him ten, then.' Mrs Lambert made a note with her slim, gold biro in her little diary, and knowing the self control her cousin was exercising in order not to break into a rage or burst into tears, she chuckled to herself.

∗

Henry opened the door of his flat in answer to an imperious ring.

'What's the matter?' asked Cliff at once.

'Nothing.'

'Yes there is, love. You're all jumpy.'

'No, I'm not.'

'Aren't you going to offer your sister a drink?'

'What'll you have?'

'The usual, ducks.'

Henry's hand trembled as he poured out the gin and took ice cubes out of the 'pineapple.'

'You are jumpy, Henrietta. Tell your sister what's the matter.'

Henry winced.

'I'd like to have my little present now, dearie. I have a date at half-past. Can I have it now?

'No, Cliff.'

'What?'

'I said, "No, Cliff".'

'You bloody well...'

'I can't get it. I haven't got it.'

Cliff rose briskly. Henry flinched.

'You fuckin' well 'ave, you lying bastard. Come on, Charlotte, gimme, gimme, gimme.' He pointed at Henry rubbing his forefinger and thumb together.

'I tell you, I can't, Cliff.' Henry glanced at the bathroom door, which was ajar.

'You can get it off your car-thief boss, Slimy Sid Stone, if you haven't got it and I know you have.'

'I haven't.'

'OK. Then I go to the police and tell them you're selling stolen cars; that's what I believe you're doing anyway. It may not be true but I've a hunch it is. I'll report you to the income tax people. I'll tell Tony's mum and dad and his girl friend you're a pouff who's corrupted Tony, gone down on your knees and put your slobbering mouth over his cock and...'

'Have another gin?' The offer sounded absurd; in fact it was an arranged signal.

The bathroom door flew open and into the living room stormed Sidney Stone's driver, a wiry little man with an Irish look, and Mr Cline, a solicitor of middle age, medium height, greying hair; his etiolated countenance suggested years shut in dark offices and stuffy court rooms. Mr Cline wore pink tinted glasses in black frames and showed surprisingly good teeth when he opened his mouth; he spoke smoothly in a mid-Atlantic accent and there was authority behind each word. Cliff collapsed into apologies after Cline's first sentence, which was, 'I suppose you are acquainted with the law of blackmail in this country, Mr Hughes, and the serious view taken of the crime...'

'I, I was only joking, I...'

'No court has any sympathy for the blackmailer, you know; at least in my experience I've never known one that has...'

'Henry, I swear. I wasn't serious, it was only...'

'What you've just said to Mr Harlow, would, even with a lenient judge, earn you about two years...'

'I wasn't blackmailing. You think I'd blackmail my old shipmate, Henry?' Cliff smiled feebly.

'I don't think anything. Surmise is not my business. Facts are.' The solicitor nodded to Stone's driver, who panther-like leapt into the bathroom and returned with a recording machine.

Cliff regarded Henry pleadingly; his bloodshot eyes betrayed his fear and his hopelessness. Quicker than the ice in the glass of gin had his menacing manner melted away.

'Turn it on,' Cline commanded. The driver obeyed and Cliff's voice relentlessly repeated the threats larded with the silly terms of endearment and hackneyed expletives that now sounded shamefully ludicrous: "The usual, ducks"; "You are jumpy, Henrietta"; "I'd like have my little present now, dearie"; "You lying bastard..."

'OK, OK!' wailed Cliff. 'That's enough. What do you want? To crucify me?'

'Quiet!' snapped the solicitor. Cliff had to listen to his miserable little blackmail scene right to the end. When the sentence beginning "I'll tell

Tony's mum and dad!" had boomed to its interrupted end, Cline said, 'Switch off. Now, Mr Hughes, would you like to hear that played in court?'

*

After Cliff had gone, defeated and frightened, Mr Cline dismissed the driver and sat on the sofa. Smiling continuously in a sort of oriental manner, he informed Henry that Stone had decided to give up the motor trade. 'He thinks the market for second-hand cars is falling off,' explained the solicitor, 'and he's pulling out of it, going into the catering; there'll be no more cars for you to sell. You can sell the car you have now and the money you get from it you can keep. Mr Stone asked me to tell you he was sorry he had no place for you at the moment. He's leaving Southampton, moving to London.' Mr Cline rose. 'However, if you have any more trouble from Hughes, let me know.' He started to pack up the recording machine, playing the tape backwards to make the conversation between Henry and Cliff sound like jungle gibberish. He removed the tape. 'I'll keep this,' he said, holding up the little coil. He put the recording apparatus into his brief case and then gave Henry his visiting card. 'Ring me if you have any trouble. I mean threats from Hughes about Mr Stone's car business, not private trouble.' He shook hands with Henry. His pink-tinted glasses acted like a mask, making it impossible to tell the colour of his eyes or their expression.

'I'd like to see Mr Stone,' said Henry.

'He's busy. He may have left for London already.'

'Have you his address, his telephone number?'

'I don't think it's worth your while trying to contact him, Mr Harlow. He's far too busy launching his new venture. Well, then goodbye! I'm pleases we got over this unsavoury business satisfactorily. By the way, there will be no charge for my services. Mr Stone will look after things. Goodbye again, Mr. Harlow.'

Part III

Henry returned to his old method of making a living; buying a car, advertising it in the local paper and selling it. Sid Stone had been right, the second-hand car market was in the doldrums. In three months Henry only sold ten cars, making a profit of not more than fifty pounds on each. He was loath to give up his way of living and in order to keep on his flat, run a car, buy gin and entertain as usual he had to draw on his savings. He could not bring himself to economise. Ever since his smuggling days, when money poured in, Henry had been prodigal. He liked eating in good restaurants and having wine with his meals; also, he would spend a good deal on Tony's substitutes in order to impress them, and on Tony when he came home on leave.

Sometimes during this affluent period Henry would take himself to London, visit a few gay pubs and a club. He had been introduced to the latter by a tall, skimpy-haired, loquacious man with a loud grand voice who had spoken to him at the Footsore Tavern. He realised that the man, who said, 'D'you know you have bedroom eyes?' was trying to pick him up. Henry did not care for older people; they reminded him of Father Hopkins. He did not mind, though, being taken to the Beckford, nor to his new acquaintance sponsoring his membership to the club.

Henry was proud of belonging to a club in London and enjoyed visiting it and pretending to be a wealthy businessman from the provinces. He experienced a most satisfying moment, when while feigning absorption in the *Evening Standard*, he had overhead Mr Whittington-Summers, the owner of the Beckford, say to a distinguished-looking

91

member in a well-cut, dark blue pinstripe, who had an imposing manner and who distorted his vowels in an upper-class way, 'Don't know much about him Godfrey. He doesn't come in often. Charles introduced him, though he told me he'd never had him. He's not rent, and apparently doesn't like older men. Pity. Good-looking, isn't he? Not your cup, perhaps. He sometimes comes in with "heaven", rather tough, absolutely "you", my dear, whom he calls Tony. I imagine he's well-off; always orders doubles; lives in Hampshire; hardly ever speaks to anyone.' These were sweet words to Henry, the sweetest he had ever heard; he often repeated some of them to himself to bolster his morale when he was down.

Henry loved the Beckford for its dim lighting. Its thick apple-green carpet, its banquette seats of yellow plush, its velvet curtains of the same hue that trailed the floor extravagantly, its shiny black bar, the stools of which had chromium arms and swivelled round. He did not notice the stains on the carpet, that the seats were grubby and needed respringing, and he had no idea of who was the portrait of the pensive, white-haired man with the sensitive face that hung above the bar, nor why it was there; he had never asked anyone because he did not like to show his ignorance. He tingled with delight as he carried two large whiskies from the bar to Tony sitting on a banquette for two, while the blue-haired man at the piano strummed 'The Man I Love.' On solitary visits Henry was content to sit alone, listen and watch. After he had heard from the deft little barman, called 'Custard' with the pale, freckled face that the distinguished gentleman who had been given information about him by the owner was Lord Rodmell, he studied the peer's features with interest. His Lordship was no beauty. His fair hair was beginning to lose out to a grey onslaught; his florid, lined face wore a disgruntled expression until it became more creased in a smile; a hacking cough made him cry out 'Damn!' and his blue eyes would fill with tears; but he was a lord and had such self-assurance that nothing, it seemed, could ruffle him. It was a big moment when Henry was able to say to Tony, 'That's Lord Rodmell over there at the bar.'

'D'you know him?'

'Not well.' Henry had twice passed the time of day with the peer and once he offered him a drink; the offer was accepted with a courteous, 'That's very good of you, my dear.'

'He keeps looking at me,' said Tony.

*

Henry found it hard to stop going to places like the Beckford after his earnings had slumped and his savings had dwindled, harder still not to entertain Tony and other friends generously, and hardest of all to admit to Mrs Lambert that the partnership with Sidney Stone, of which he had spoken with such confidence and pride, had ended. He had to tell her something. Finally, after much pondering, he invented the story that Stone had gone to California. 'His brother has a big supermarket chain up and down the state,' he explained. 'Mr Stone wants me to go out there and manage one of his stores.' Trying not to sound enthusiastic, Mrs Lambert said, 'That would be a wonderful opportunity, Henry.' 'I don't fancy going so far away,' the young man replied with undue emphasis. 'I see,' said the old lady, not understanding at all and wondering if she should feel touched.

*

In the summer of 1956 James came home on holiday from Beirut. Having picked up an undemanding teaching post, he had decided to prolong his sojourn in Lebanon. One weekend when Donald was staying at Gorsebanks and Henry was also there, James, accustomed to using terms of endearment in front of his friend, let slip a 'Thank you, my dear' to Henry for guiding him out of the garage.

'Of course he realises you're queer,' said Donald. 'Didn't you notice his smile after you said "my dear"?'

'I wasn't looking at him.'

'What's Henry doing now?'

'Something to do with cars, I suppose.'

'If you were attracted to him your attitude towards him would be different.'

'Perhaps.'

Donald was right. If James had been sure that Henry was queer he would have acted towards him in a more sympathetic way; as it was, he was distant, and having little in common with him he found his company boring. Mrs Lambert was afraid that James's coldness would make Henry feel that he was only at Gorsebanks on sufferance. She was anxious for James to approve of Henry. 'Do be nice to Henry,' she begged James more than once.

Donald left after supper on the Sunday. It was early July and his school had not yet broken up. When he had gone, James, feeling he ought to make an effort and the 'be nice to Henry,' suggested a walk on the cliffs. 'It's a lovely evening.'

'I must return,' said Henry.

'Return tomorrow. What does it matter?'

'Would your mother mind if I stayed?'

'Don't be silly, Henry. You can stay as long as you like.'

'I don't want to be a nuisance. Your mother has been so good to me.'

At the top of the road in which Gorsebanks stood screened by a high hedge, they crossed the Overcliff Drive and joined the asphalt path along the top of the cliffs. Durlston Head was visible and so were Swanage Bay, Old Harry Rocks and Studland. Elderly men and women, some in couples, some alone, were giving their dogs an evening walk. James wondered in which shelter his father had found Henry's mother. Was Henry aware that they were strolling near the spot where Dr Lambert had discovered Bessie Harlow, pregnant and dying twenty-eight years ago? In the distance a Salvation Army band was pounding out a hymn.

'Bournemouth Bay compares favourably with other bays in the world, don't you think?' James did not mean to sound pompous or pedantic; he found it hard to be natural when making conversation with Henry. 'If one travels a lot one is apt to disparage the beauties of one's own land, don't you think?' Henry made no comment. James went on, 'But as for the town of Bournemouth, there's not much to be said for it, is there? It's dull. Don't you agree, Henry, it's dull.'

'"Clear before us through the darkness, gleams and burns the guiding light..."'

The words of the hymn became audible as they approached the Salvation Army gathering.

'Yes, it is dull, James.'

'Is Southampton dull?'

'Less so than Bournemouth.'

'"One the object of our journey, One the faith which never tires..."'

'London's best, though,' said Henry.

James did not look at his companion, who was several inches taller than he. 'Best for what?'

'Best for bars.'

'What bars do you go to?'

They were near the circle of earnestly playing and fervently singing Salvationists; the congregation amounted to about ten old ladies and three old men, one of whom, white haired and with a stick, owned a fat Labrador, which twitched its ears each time a diminutive, poke-bonneted sergeant, emitted a high note. James glanced twice at a young, blond trumpeter.

'"Onward therefore pilgrim brothers, Onward with the Cross our aid…"'

'Well,' said Henry, 'I go to the Fitzroy sometimes, and I also belong to a club.'

'Which one?'

'The Beckford,' admitted Henry, as a City Broker might say 'Boodles'.

'So do I.'

'You belong to the Beckford?'

'Yes, have done for years. Rarely go there now. Don't like the crowd much and that dreadful owner. Did you think I was queer?'

'Oh, don't say "queer", James, say "gay". Yes, I did think so after I saw you and Donald in that hotel bar in Bournemouth; and this morning so camp you were, calling me "my dear" as you were backing out of the garage. Did you think I was gay?'

'I wondered. Donald and I wondered when you came into that hotel bar and swept that beauty away, whom I'd been admiring.'

'That was Tony. He's been my boyfriend for some time now.'

'Quite a dish. My mother told me you had a girlfriend.'

'I made that up. Tony's in the army now.'

'Do you think my mother guesses about me?'

'She's pretty shrewd, your mother is.'

'Whatever possessed you to blurt out that story of the man who tried to pick you up on the ship outside the Austin Reed shop at tea that day?'

'It was to make your mother think I wasn't gay. I wanted her to think I didn't know what the man wanted. It wasn't long after I'd brought an ever so gay friend of mine called Cliff down for the weekend. Upset your mother he did, so camp he was. I should never have taken him to Gorsebanks. It was wrong of me. I told the story about the man to throw your mother off the scent.'

'Did you let yourself get picked up by him? Did you let him buy you a shirt?'

'No, course not.'

They had climbed a dune covered with marram grass and were looking west at the piers of Boscombe and Bournemouth. James switched his gaze to Henry's profile. He now regarded Henry in a different light. The young man was really not at all bad looking. James liked the way the tip of his nose bent downwards slightly when the corners of his turned up. Now the nose was straight but should Henry smile...

Henry regarded James. 'What's the matter?' he asked suspiciously.

'Nothing. I was just admiring the view,' replied James gazing into Henry's large gooseberry eyes.

Henry cleared his throat. 'Your mother's been very good to me,' he remarked. 'Your aunt doesn't like me though.'

Embarrassed, James took the hint. 'Poor Florence! She ought to have married.'

'She could hardly expect to with a nose like that, could she?'

'In fact she had two suitors. She had to reject both of them in order to look after her mother, a tiresome *malade imaginaire*, who, when there was a possibility of Florence leaving home, feigned illness. The second suitor was a Lord Rodmell.'

'Lord Rodmell? I know him,' said Henry, proudly.

'He died years ago in a motor smash, soon after he was married, not to Florence of course.'

'But I see him at the Beckford sometimes.'

'That must be the son of Florence's Lord Rodmell. How funny!'

'Do you know him?'

'No,' replied James. 'Is he a special friend of yours?'

Henry laughed. 'He must be fifty. I go for beauty, James. Strictly for youth and beauty, see? Tony's what I like.'

'Tell me about him,' said James, trying not to sound snubbed...

Henry's description of his affair with Tony and of the young man's talents smacked of hyperbole, as did his account of Cliff's blackmail attempt. 'I called the police,' Henry fantasised, 'and two detectives hid behind curtains, and when he started to threaten me, they jumped out and arrested him. There was a case. He was sent to gaol. Awful to do that to a shipmate. He was the one I brought to Gorsebanks. In this life, it's sink or swim; one had to keep one's head above water, you know James.'

'I think it would be better if you kept your head *on* the water.'

'What d'you mean?'

'Go back to sea.'

'They wouldn't have me back.'

'There are other lines.'

*

James drove up to London, where, on the eve of his departure for Beirut, he took his airman friend, Alec, to the theatre. When at a certain moment in the play, the leading actor, a famous American film star, suddenly whipped off his shirt, Alec's penetrating Midland voice cut through the heavy silence in the auditorium, 'Oh James, I didn't realise that 'e 'ad such a luvly body.' A few heads turned in the stalls; James shifted in his seat and rubbed his chin.

James liked Alec, but was not in love with him. The two had little in common when not in bed together. He dared not take Alec to his club or to a hotel, so he encroached on the hospitality of a friend with a flat in Bayswater. This meant making do with a narrow divan in the sitting-room; better though to run the risk of falling on the floor then to be sneaked on by a prying hotel employee. James was apprehensive. There had been some trials of homosexuals recently involving just such a liaison as himself and Alec. Life was far less oppressive in Lebanon, where the authorities did not care about sexual venialities whatever form they took. James was afraid to live in England at least while his mother was alive; the thought of the shame a scandal would bring upon him and Mrs Lambert made him go hot and cold.

'I daren't so much as glance at anyone when I'm in England,' remarked Laurence, a close friend of James's in Beirut. 'A smile might get you arrested or beaten up, a wink could mean a prison sentence. I go along looking ahead, avoiding eye contact with anyone. As for peeing in a public loo, I wouldn't do anything so foolhardy. The loos are full of *agents provocateurs* hiding in the cubicles and peeping out at you. My knees shake so badly when I'm in the stalls that nothing comes out.'

*

One morning that autumn Mrs Lambert's habitual perusal of the obituary column in *The Times* did not go unrewarded: Father Hopkins had died at the age of fifty-nine. Thinking that Henry would like to attend the funeral, Mrs Lambert wrote to him immediately, but he did not even send flowers. At the old lady's mention of the priest's demise the following Saturday, Henry said no more than he was sorry and then changed the subject to that of his present predicament. Mrs Lambert mistook her godson's reticence about the deceased priest for grief. During periods of depression Henry would curse Hopkins for seducing him and for curtailing his education; he never dispelled his godmother's notion that the Father was a fine good man, to whom eternal gratitude should be owed.

A few months after Hopkins's death, the Rev. Cyril Willingdon-Russett appealed for contributions towards the purchase of a plot of land adjacent to the Home for the making of a Father Hopkins memorial garden. Mrs Lambert posted off a small cheque and recommended Henry to do likewise. 'After all,' she reminded her godson, 'he looked after you for so many years and prepared you for confirmation.' Grudgingly Henry sent ten pounds. He would have liked to send less; he feared a smaller amount might give the impression of indigence.

It was difficult for Henry to admit failure. Something happened in the shipping office at Southampton where he had been applying for readmission to the company that upset him so much that he drove straight to Bournemouth to seek solace from Mrs Lambert.

'Each week,' he told her, 'the man in the office advised me to come back the following week. I went. It's now nearly two months. Seven times. Then this morning after I'd waited more than an hour in the queue of the applicants the man turned over my card, pushed it in my face. On the back was a cutting of the newspaper account of when I tried to board the *Queen Elizabeth* without permission. "D'you think we'd employ you again?" he said.'

'How beastly! Henry, I am sorry.' Mrs Lambert was entirely on the side of her protégé. 'Why not try another company?'

'That's what James said. But I wanted to get back onto one of the *Queens*.'

'He was right. Go to London, Henry, and see if you can get accepted by another line.'

Henry went and was accepted.

Florence was caustic when her cousin told her that Henry had gone back to sea. 'I'm surprised any company agreed to have him after his long absence from the merchant navy, and such a good company too. I'm not in the least surprised that his car-trade business or whatever it was petered out. How could he have expected to succeed with no education and no acumen.'

'He has quite a lot of acumen,' said Mrs Lambert. 'By the way he'll be going to Sydney. Shall I give him Robert's address?'

'No, Margaret, I forbid you to.'

Mrs Lambert chuckled. She knew full well that the mere suggestion of Henry meeting Florence's brother would infuriate her cousin.

*

In Sydney, instead of meeting Florence's brother, whom he had no desire to see (if he had seen him he would have found that Australia had knocked the Branson pretentiousness and snobbery out of him and he was quite unlike his sister) Henry ran into Cliff in a bar. Their eyes clashed once without giving a sign of recognition, both pretending they had not noticed each other; then, after a few minutes, their curiosity acted as a magnet that drew them together. It was Cliff who moved towards his ex-friend, former accomplice, and when they were next each other Henry smiled a weak but friendly smile. Cliff was fatter and beginning to bald. He was now thirty-five.

'You must be on that pre-First-World-Ward barge that limped into port this morning like a diseased whore,' said Cliff.

'You're in the new one, I suppose.'

'Trust your sister to be on the queen of the fleet. I'm a waitress in *first* class. What are you Henry, a plate washer in the gallery?'

'I'm in tourist, a waiter.'

'On that miserable piece of floating scrap? Right for the breakers, she is. You should get on my ship. Why don't you sign off yours when you get home and apply for a job on mine?'

'I might.' It was good to see Cliff again, in spite of all the pain and anxiety knowing him had caused. He had loved Cliff, who had made him laugh, and Henry not being of a humorous temperament (he could never tell a joke, rarely see one) did not laugh easily. Henry had also hated Cliff. It was now two years since they had seen each other. Henry was prepared to forgive him. Neither of them mentioned the past. Cliff had been utterly vile. Henry had struck back and humiliated him. Henry was not vengeful. He had acted in desperation. Now the less said the better, and Cliff might be useful.

Henry said, 'There's something I want to ask you.'

Cliff swallowed and guardedly said, 'What?'

'Have you any drag?'

Cliff sighed. 'Oh, dolly, I love you for that. Yes, ducks, course I have.'

'I haven't and...'

'You need some? Naturally. A girl must dress as the occasion demands. And on our ship – I don't know about yours – on our ship the occasion often does demand that one slips into something loose and fetching. Henriette, I can see you in blue, sky blue. I know just the place.'

With Cliff's help Henry bought some female attire in a Sydney emporium. 'It's for his sister,' explained Cliff to the puzzled sales girl in the dress department. While Henry was looking diffidently at a row of frocks, Cliff put a hand on his shoulder and whispered, 'I was a beastess. Sorry. I wasn't myself.' Then, aloud to the shopgirl, he said, 'It's for his twin sister, you see, who happens to be the same size.'

Henry took a blue dress off the rail.

'You'd better try it on,' advised Cliff.

'No!'

'You see,' said Cliff to the girl, 'if he tries it on, he'll know it'll fit his sister.'

'Well,' said the salesgirl doubtfully. 'I suppose he could.'

'No, its not necessary,' said Henry. 'I'll have this one.'

The two stewards went on to buy a brassiere, three pairs of nylon stockings ('Will I need three pairs?' asked Henry. 'Stockings get torn to shreds, don't they?' Cliff appealed to the salesgirl, who nodded readily) a pair of black, high-heeled shoes, some costume jewellery (plastic pearl drops for the ears, a necklace and a brooch in the same material) and three little lace handkerchiefs. Henry had tried to resist the last item.

'Perhaps the most important article in a woman's trousseau,' Cliff expostulated, flapping his hand and then daintily dabbing each nostril; the girl behind the counter agreed.

Henry bought the handkerchiefs and refused to get a handbag.

Outside the shop he collapsed into nervous laughter. 'Oh God, Cliff, how could you be so serious? I nearly died.'

'My dear, shopping is a serious matter. Anyway, you were mad not to purchase a handbag.'

'I don't need a handbag.'

'You don't need one? Huh! Where, I ask you, are you going to put your cosmetics and other things? You can't carry them around in your hands. A dress has no pockets. You *must* have a handbag.'

Henry agreed to get one, not in the same shop to which he dared not return. He bought a little, cheap velvet evening handbag in another shop.

Each of the three other stewards in Henry's cabin possessed a drag outfit, so Henry was able to indulge in that shopper's joy of showing off his purchases.

'I'm not sure about the dress,' said Madge, who had been christened Mark by the parents. 'Try it on and let's see.' Henry did and his shipmates appraised the result gravely: they declared the dress to be too short and the brassiere in need of more padding. 'A blond wig would do wonders to your face, Henrietta,' said "Eileen", a pensive finger to his lips. If James had seen the lanky Henry in his ill-fitting, blue dress with bulging breast, lips oozing with lipstick, eyelashes plastered with mascara, toppling along on his high heels, he would have doubled up with laughter. In fact he did laugh a great deal when the following summer Henry told him about his feminine get-up.

'When do you wear it?' James asked Henry during their after-dinner stroll along the cliff paths. It was on these walks rather than in Gorsebanks that the two men talked intimately. 'Do you put it on every night like dressing for dinner?'

'No. Only at the parties and smoke concerts. We have parties in the Pig, that's the canteen.'

'What happens at the parties?'

'Some of the stewards do numbers. There's one – Charlotte – who does ever such a good imitation of Marlene Dietriech singing "Falling in Love again." He has a fabulous wig. Cost pounds it did, made of real hair.'

'Do you do a number, Henry?' asked James.

'No, I dance and ply my man with drink, get him into a corner and, and oh, once you get a few double gins down him he's a pushover, James'

'Where do you go for sex?'

'The forecastle head. Only place. And that can be difficult if it's busy there or there's been a heavy dew. I usually get my chicken dinner, though.'

'D'you have one friend or many?' James was fascinated by Henry's life on board.

'One, if possible. This last trip I had a lovely plate washer from the galley. Real lovely boy he was.'

'Did you go ashore with him at Bombay or Freemantle or somewhere?'

'No. Once on land he went for women.'

'So you won't see him in London or anywhere before you sail again.'

'It was just a shipboard romance, confined to the high seas.'

'Not a love affair, like the one you had with Tony?'

'No.' Henry replied. 'You see, James, I like men. Gay people don't interest me. Bread and bread make a dull sandwich. I'm strictly a lady, see?'

*

Because he had heard so much about Henry, Laurence, a Beirut friend, had worked up quite an interest in the young man. As soon as James had returned to Lebanon, he asked, 'What's the latest about your mother's protégé?'

'He wears drag.'

'Heavens! At Gorsebanks? What does your mother say?'

'Not at Gorsebanks, on board at drag parties. The gay stewards wear drag to attract the men and they enjoy camping around.'

'Drag doesn't attract me; it puts me off, if anything.'

'Me too. Henry keeps on about not liking gay people.'

'That's to ward you off,' said Laurence.

'I haven't dared make another pass. Bread and bread makes a dull sandwich, Henry says. He also declares, "I'm strictly a lady, see." What can that mean?'

'It could only mean one thing, I should have thought,' said Laurence. 'It's surprising that the merchant navy has any ships afloat with all the drinking, camping and dragging up that goes on, not to mention the "fun" and "games" on the forecastle head.'

Henry always sent James a sailing list that gave the dates when his ship would be at various ports of call and James did his best to squeeze out a letter twice a voyage – 'Do write', his mother, who wrote to every port, urged. 'It makes such a difference his having letters. Henry's replies to James's letters were intermittent.

'Dear James,

Many thanks for your welcome letter. I'm glad you're still liking Beirut. I don't think I like those Arabs. Their fierce and dangerous what I've seen of them. Wouldn't trust them, James, and those that come on board at Port Said are a cheating lot, liars, have to watch them, keep your cabin locked. Pinch anything. Some go for the Lascars on board. I don't. Give me a nice English man any time. Hope to see you in August but this ship is to go on cruises so won't have much free time unless I sign off and don't want to do that now I'm first class on the company's flagship. Ought to make good money on the cruises as cruise passengers tip well. And now I have two tables. Have a nice friend Terry on this trip. He is my assistant. Aussies are awful tippers. Hardly give anything after the long voyage to Australia. The headwaiter on this ship is an old friend of mine. He got me the job. Forgive this awful letter and my awful writing.

> Love and be good (don't), Henry.'

Henry's courtesy and efficiency made him popular with the passengers. He was adept at dealing with old ladies, who adored him, unlike some waiters, he treated them considerately, remembering their special needs, even when he knew their tips would be small. His reliability and conscientiousness were noticed and reported upon; after his second round trip to Australia, Cliff used his influence to get him transferred to first class.

Responsibility, liver trouble and a feeling of remorse about the past had changed Cliff. Occasionally he let fly a salvo from his arsenal of vituperation; Clara had gone and Cliff was now a stout, balding, sober person. He worked diligently, no longer overdrank and never misbehaved with any of the crew. 'I've given all that up,' he told Henry. 'I've had enough sex to last a lifetime. Not long after we met in Sydney – two years ago, was it – I collapsed. It was my liver, swollen to the size of a balloon, it was, the doctor said. Only cure, cut down the alc... I have. A few beers and a glass or two of wine is all I have now. And, funny. I don't seem to want any sex. Christ! That me the wildest of them all should go off it, but I have. D'you know I have nightmares sometimes about the things I did, way back. I was crazy. I don't need to tell you. Think of how I carried on at your godmother's house and in Southampton after we'd left the Lizzie. I was drunk half the time. And the way I behaved to you. All that kind of thing is over. But don't worry. I'm not going to try and stop you from having fun, but you're not to let me down. I asked for you, dolly. Don't forget I got you here. There's ninety under me in the dining-room and everyone's got to do their job properly. In the dining room you're a waiter; in the Pig you can be the Queen of Sheba for all I care, but no camping on duty and no chatting up your latest crush either.'

These word were spoken to Henry in Cliff's private cabin. It was the privilege of the headwaiter first class to have a single outside cabin to himself in the first class part of the ship. Cliff ruled his subordinates with his abrasive tongue, guile and severity. 'I will not have that in my dining-room,' he would then say, eyes blazing, to an old hand, who had pinched a young waiter's plate of roast beef. 'If you don't trip very carefully, Dulcie you'll be back in bloody tourist before the voyage's out.' To the passengers he was polite and charming, but his manner had the firmness of authority behind it. He was feared by the waiters and respected by the passengers. Henry learnt a lot from him.

After two voyages, Henry was promoted to the inner circle of tables, a post given to the best waiters. He heard that the captain attended the Communion service on board and he pretended to Mrs Lambert that he did so too. 'I always see the captain at service on Sundays,' he wrote to her. She told James this in one of her letters. 'It's a joy to me,' she wrote, 'that his religion means something to him. It's a relief to know that the Home was not a mistake, that it gave him the background that your father and I wanted him to have. Father Hopkins must have been a very good man. Did Henry tell you that he sent £10 in response to an appeal to raise money for a memorial garden to Father Hopkins? It just shows how grateful he was to the Father and how he…'

*

For as long as James could remember Mrs Lambert's letters had been written in the same careful evenly formed words running straight across the small sheet of unlined writing paper embossed at the top with the Gorsebanks address. The sight of the familiar neat writing on the blue envelopes on hall tables, under doors, in the hand of a clerk at some Poste Restante, in the clutches of a bank employee, an Arab servant had often made James feel apprehensive. Had some misdemeanour been found out? Even now the apprehension remained, mostly because of Alec.

When in England the previous summer, Alec had telephoned Gorsebanks while he was out and Mrs Lambert, in the absence of her companion, Miss Phillips, had struggled to the phone on her stick. 'Someone rang you, James,' she said in an anxious voice. 'Oh yes?' replied James. 'Who was it?' 'He just said Alec. He sounded quite common.' James blushed and turned to look out of the window at a trellis-work arch which bore a so-called blue rambler that had, according to his mother's plan, successfully entwined itself with a clematis; the clematis was over but the rose was in bloom. 'What did he say his name was? Alec? Oh Alec!' he said with sudden unconvincing apprehension. That must be the fellow I met last year on my way to Genoa to catch the boat to Beirut. Staying at the same hotel in Cannes. One meets all sorts of people on the Cote d'Azur these day.' He paused. 'I say, that blue rambler has done well. I'd hardly call it blue, though.' It was not the first time he had made that remark. Very quietly, Mrs Lambert said, 'No.' The negative was heavily loaded with suspicion and made James feel uncomfortable.

Therefore the neat hand on the blue envelope even in the Lebanese spring, caused a tremble of misgiving: had Alec rung up again?

Suddenly the writing became wobbly and ran unsteadily over the blue paper, the sentences drooping down the page: 'I don't seem to hold my pen properly. It's so silly. A temporary affliction I'm sure. I'll be alright when it gets warmer. We are having such a cold spring, though the blossom has been lovely.' One day the blue envelope was addressed in Miss Phillip's alien hand and the scrawl was alarming: 'Don't worry but I've asked Mrs Jackson to take me into her nursing home next door. I'm not very well but I'm sure I'll be all right by the time you are back.' And then came a telegram from Florence. Bourgeois parsimony had made her put just two words, which the Lebanese post office had misspelled to read, 'Com Hoem'. To James the message looked odd, unreal, as if his aunt had written it in Double Dutch. He flew home at once. Mrs Lambert died five hours before James telephoned Gorsebanks from Waterloo Station.

*

That May was inclement, Sleet destroyed the blossom on the magnolia tree outside the study, in which Florence and James sat. Florence was tearful. Before James arrived she had been in touch with an undertaker and arranged for the funeral. She had read the Will, a short document which left everything to James apart from a few minor bequests to charities, including one to Henry's Home, a legacy of five hundred pounds to Florence and another of the same amount to Henry.

'I thought she might have left more to Henry. She was so fond of him.' With the toe of her shoe she stroked the back of her dozing Cairn. 'And she never left anything to wizzie-wozzems, did she, darling?'

James made an indeterminate noise in his throat and crossed his legs.

'I didn't expect anything at all,' Florence went on weepily. 'I am very grateful to have five hundred pounds. It'll come in useful. You'll be a wealthy man, James.'

'I don't know. Death duties will take a lot.'

'Not all. There's that farm in Surrey too. What'll you do with that?'

'Keep it. It's let.'

'And this house?'

'Sell it.'

'You do think it was all right only to have sent Henry a letter and not a cable?'

'What could he do? He's half way between Bombay and Freemantle, according to the sailing list.'

'I've never written to him before,' said Florence. 'It's surprising,' she went on, 'your mother didn't leave him more.' Florence's watery eyes overflowed, her face reddened and became suffused; she stuffed her little handkerchief between her false teeth and unsuccessfully stifled a sob.

*

James hated admitting it, even to himself, that was some truth in the dictum that no man feels free until both his parents are dead. He gave Donald three dry martinis instead of the usual pre-prandial glass of sherry, and at dinner they drank a bottle of Burgundy between them, except for one half-glass bashfully accepted by Miss Phillips. He wrote to Alec at his RAF camp inviting him to stay, suggesting he should telephone and reverse the charges; he bought a new Jaguar in spite of his having left behind in Beirut a one-year-old Vauxhall; he went up to London more often than had been his habit on previous visits; he ordered three suits from his Mayfair tailor, two more than the customary annual quota.

Florence was summoned to go and nurse her elder sister, Gladys, who, after a second stroke, had become bedridden. James felt freer than ever, although Florence hadn't moved into Gorsebanks, she was a frequent visitor; she would arrive without warning at any hour in the day.

James gave a weekend house party at Gorsebanks consisting of Donald, Alec and Hussein, a Persian student whom James had known in Teheran and who was studying in London. Miss Phillips was surprised when no one except Donald, who went to church, got up before ten-thirty on the Sunday morning, and shocked when she discovered Alec and Hussein in James's bed in the afternoon, while the two older men were walking off their lunch along the cliff paths. 'A little too much wine, that is all, Miss Phillips.' James explained, trying to pass off the incident as a matter of no consequence. He was cross with Alec and Hussein because it was not on the programme for them to bed down together. That weekend James had to face a truth: young men often prefer other young men to those approaching middle-age.

'Of course they do,' said Donald, the celibate, on their second walk that day, after Alex and Hussein had returned to London together. James knew that Alec had to return to his camp, but it had been agreed that Hussein would stay till the Monday and he would go to London with James in the brand new Jaguar.

Miss Phillips had another shock that afternoon: she caught James in the kitchen filling the kettle from the hot tap, a more serious solecism, it seemed, than catching the two young men in *flagrant délit*.

At tea Hussein had coolly announced that he would be accompanying Alec to London that evening. The comely Persian maintained that he had just remembered a class which he ought to attend the next morning. To James's dismay Alec seemed delighted to have the exotic, swarthy Hussein with the gazelle eyes as a travelling companion.

'D'you mean to say,' he asked James, squeezing a juicy finger of misembrianthemum he had broken off,' that from now on we'll only get people for money?'

'Unless they're gerontophiles,' replied Donald.

'How does one find a gerontophile?'

'They are not uncommon in the Far East, I believe.'

'The Far East? Will we have to go there for satisfaction? But to return to Alec, do you think he went to bed with Hussein because he was attracted or because he was forced to? Hussein is quite strong. I know.'

'Because he was attracted.'

James snapped off a blade of marron grass and put it between his teeth. 'Am I old enough to be a father figure?' he asked his friend after they had walked the hundred yards between two shelters in silence.

'Oh yes.'

'How smug you are, Donald! You who never have sex and therefore never experience any of its complications, its problems.'

'Or its delights,' said Donald, wistfully.

*

'Isn't she beautiful!' exclaimed Henry. He was referring to his ship, which in the dock did indeed did look fine from the ferry at Tilbury, on which he and James were crossing to Gravesend. James had gone to meet the ship, which had just returned from Australia. It was the first time James had seen Henry since Mrs Lambert's death, and, knowing that Henry would miss her greatly, he wanted to reassure him that in a sort of way he was willing to take her place. 'I want you to feel, Henry,' James told him, 'that I am a sort of relation.' Night had fallen. They were motoring through Kent when James said this; it was a statement made more easily in the dark. 'By the way, I've put Gorsebanks on the market.'

'You're selling Gorsebanks?'

So shocked did Henry seem that James laughed, 'Why not?'

'You were born there.'

James laughed again. 'It's hardly a great family seat, Henry. Built in 1908, it's comfortable, but useless to me and besides I hate Bournemouth.'

'What will you do with all the furniture, and the china your mother loved so, and other stuff?'

'Store the best, sell the rest.'

'Where will you live?'

'Oh, I'll wander for a few years. I still have a contract with the school in Beirut. Next year I want to go to Japan.'

'James, could you put some of my things in store with yours?'

'Of course.'

'Your mother did say that all the things in my bedroom were mine.'

They motored on. James sat rather proudly at the wheel of the Jaguar; twice he asked Henry if he liked it.

'It's a lovely job, James. You might have done better to get a year-old car, though. These cars depreciate so. Drive it out of the garage new and at once you drop several hundred.' After a while, Henry said, 'May I ask you something James?'

'What?'

'I have to give the company the name of my next of kin. May I put your name and say you're a cousin?'

James hesitated and having done so immediately wished he had not; he feared that Henry might interpret his hesitation to think he disliked the idea of being officially registered as a relation of a steward. He said, after a pause, 'Of course you may,' but too late.

'It's only that I have to put down someone. I've always put your mother's name before. You won't have to do anything. It'll cost you nothing.'

'Of course put my name.' James cursed his failure to have agreed spontaneously. He changed the subject by mentioning the Alec-Hussein weekend. 'Miss Phillips found them in bed together while Donald and I were out for a walk.'

'What did she say?'

'Not much, actually. It seemed to matter more to her that they'd been in my bed than in a bed in one of the spare rooms. "Those friends of yours," she said, "have been playing about in your bedroom. I don't know what your mother would have said." God! What would she have said? I told Miss Phillips that they had a bit too much too drink at lunch – although Hussein had drunk nothing but water. Fortunately Miss Phillips is completely naïve. I'm sure the fact they were having sex never entered her head. I was furious with Alex and more furious still when he and Hussein went back to London together. Donald says that at my age I can't expect to have lovers for free.'

'That's right,' agreed Henry, seriously, as if James had uttered a great truth. 'I used to wonder how it was that fat, bald Jews with hairy hands got hold of beautiful young blonds. Now I know. They pay and money can buy anything and anyone.'

'I've been meaning to ask you, Henry, have you ever been to bed with a woman?'

'No, have you?'

'Yes, but why haven't you?'

'I never wanted to, James. Never thought of it, and you have?'

'Yes, several times, but eventually I realised that I didn't like it much.'

'I should think not.'

Florence's sister died. She did better out of her sister's estate that she had done out of her cousin's: she was left the income from a trust of fifty-thousand pounds and a car, a Morris Minor. She had always longed to drive; her slender resources and Mrs Lambert's discouragement had prevented her. Now she had a car and an increased income.

Due to summer cruises Henry's ship was based in Southampton and he was able to visit Gorsebanks more often – he had given up the flat he used to rent in the port. James, wanting to make up for the lack of warmth he had shown on the journey from Tilbury, encouraged him to come. Although Henry was pleasant enough to look at, his company palled after a while. Sex was about the only subject they had in common, and while yarns about experiences with shipmates had at the first telling been diverting, when heard for the third or fourth time, they were tedious, especially since Henry spoke enthusiastically and he did not titillate his listener with any earthy details.

'But what exactly do you do?' James would ask, irritably.

'He was a man and I was strictly a lady.'

'So he fucked you?'

'Oh James, you are rude!'

'Well, did he?'

'I don't go in for that.'

'What do you do then?' James asked impatiently.

'Oh, I like my chicken dinners and you've no idea, how many men, real men, will turn over after a few drinks.'

'That's not much use to you, is it, your being strictly a lady?'

'Oh James, you are dreadful!'

So James and Henry talked, rather unsatisfactorily, of sex on their summer evening walks along the cliffs, and sometimes of money. When Henry mentioned the latter, James became even less interested and because of the trivial amount his mother had left her godson embarrassed at the same time.

'Will you now stay in the Merchant Navy, make it your career?' he asked Henry one of these walks.

'No. I don't want to become one of those tired old queens who go on till they drop. You see them come on board, their tongues hanging out for a cheap drink and a bit of sex. Dead beat they are with their glazed eyes, their dyed hair, their faces thick with slap.' He spoke with contempt and added vehemently, 'They're pathetic.'

'Couldn't you become a chief steward or something?'

'Chief steward? That's not much.'

'Henry, if you want to leave the sea, I'll help you with whatever you want to do: go into a small business or something. But first you must save. I'll match what you save, thousand for thousand.'

'We could be partners,' said Henry, interested in the idea and quite excited by it. 'We might share a house one day, James.'

James said nothing.

'I know I can make money. I know I'm good at selling.'

*

Apart from Henry's visits, rendezvous with prospective buyers of Gorsebanks, paper work over Mrs Lambert's estate, the sorting out of things to be kept, things to be sold (among some papers James found a letter from the editor of a London newspaper in reply to one from Mrs Lambert in which she had, it seemed, protested about the prominence given to a homosexual case – had she imagined her son being involved in a scandal?) one of the bugbears of that summer was Florence and her car.

Before going to nurse her dying sister, Florence had let her house for three months, and when the melancholy task was done she had nowhere to go and nothing to do; a nephew was winding up her sister's estate. James agreed to invite Florence to stay at Gorsebanks and to drive her car from Cheltenham to Bournemouth. 'I'll be able to housekeep for you. It's an ill wind,' Florence said. 'I've got "L" plates so I can drive part of the way.'

Florence's driving was so frightening, and her requests for James to take her on practice runs so constant that the rest of the summer at Gorsebanks, the last he would ever spend there, was ruined; only for a brief month had he revelled in being alone and in command of his mother's house. Miss Phillips was self-effacing and uninterfering, except when really provoked as she had been when she caught James filling the kettle from the hot water tap and surprised Alec and Hussein in his bed. After the reproachful look she had given James in the kitchen, there was no likelihood of his repeating the solecism, and now that Florence had

111

ensconced herself at Gorsebanks there could be no opportunity for any misbehaviour.

James tried to invent excuses to avoid giving Florence driving lessons: paper work over his mother's estate was one, having to wait in for a prospective purchaser was another, and a third, the weakest, was suffering from a 'splitting headache'. Nevertheless there was often a spare half hour. 'Just up and down the road, please James,' she would beg, and off they would jerk, stalling up the road towards the cliffs in the Morris Minor, making the little car leap forward only to come to a standstill a moment later after gear grindings, a 'Damn!' from Florence and a groan from James. They would shoot in the Overcliff Drive narrowly to miss an oncoming car. The screeching of tyres and the hooting of horns that such a foolhardy manoeuvre caused were unusual sounds in the quite residential district; sometimes there would be an angry shout as well, and once or twice a barrack-room insult was hurled. Florence, provoked, would exclaim, 'People have forgotten there is such a thing as "the courtesy of the road".'

Henry got two weeks holiday when the cruises came to an end and he spent them at Gorsebanks. 'I'm awfully sorry, Aunt Florence,' James said one afternoon, 'but I can't take you out now. Someone's coming to look over the house. Why don't you ask Henry?' She did. Suddenly Florence, for the first time since she met him, behaved reasonably to Henry, actually talking to him at meals instead of ignoring him and only addressing her remarks to James or Miss Phillips. Henry saw through this change of attitude. 'She's nice to me because she wants something,' he told James. After giving Florence three lessons, he said, 'James, must I take her out? She's terrifying. She'll give me a nervous breakdown.'

'You're a great help, Henry.'

'I only do it for you, James. Just as I was nice to her because of your mother.'

Henry went on to tell James the truth about Father Hopkins, how the priest had seduced him and when Henry had refused to grant further favours prevented him from going to a secondary school.

'What a swine! I always thought you liked Hopkins and that he had been good to you.'

'I said so because of your mother, James. I didn't want to disappoint her. She believed that Father Hopkins and the Home was perfect. I couldn't tell her the true facts, could I now?'

That summer of death and inheritance, licence and independence, followed by interference and arrogance, terminated with the sale of Gorsebanks to a Mrs Prestcott from Wolverhampton. 'We like the garden,' Mrs Prestcott said in her flat voice. 'It's a garden we can get cracking on and make into something.' James did not tell her that his mother, with the aid of gardeners, had spent forty-seven years planning and altering the lay-out and caring for the trees, shrubs, bulbs, lawns, flowers, vegetables and fruit bushes and the end of her life had been pleased with her operation.

When that memorable summer was over Henry returned to his ship, James to Beirut, Miss Phillips to her one-room flat and Florence to her bungalow.

Florence had progressed but little with her driving and since she dreaded being told she would never pass the test, she was afraid of having lessons from a professional instructor. The Morris Minor remained in her garage. Sometimes she would sit in the car and sob, especially after she had given herself a large gin and orange.

Part IV

The following June James went on a tour of the Far East. In Tokyo he was completely knocked off his feet, not by one of those summer typhoons, but by a force compelling: the charms of a ballet dancer. Minoru was the most exciting person he had ever met. So captivated was James that all he could think about when he got back to Beirut was of returning to Japan. This he succeeded in doing the following year, negotiating through an acquaintance an appointment at a university in the capital.

Meanwhile Cliff left the sea to obey a summons for help from an ailing uncle in Sydney. The vacant post of head waiter first class was filled by Henry, who was delighted with the accommodation that went with the job; having a cabin to himself made all the difference to life on board. He had not liked being under an obligation to Cliff, albeit the past had been forgiven, yet he was grateful to his old shipmate for having aided him. Cliff had only helped. Henry's promotion had largely been to his own capability.

Henry decorated his cabin with some of his treasures. There were painted plaster heads of 'Prince' Monolulu, the black racing tipster, the Mexican peasant and the Red Indian Chief from his old Southampton flat, a modern Turkish plate with Allah on it in Arabic script (a present from James which he didn't much like) and a water-colour of Dartmoor. The last a triptych in a wide golden frame which used to hang in his bedroom at Gorsebanks – the Victorian painting looked singularly out of place in the white-walled cabin with its wash-basin, mirror, water pipes and air-conditioning ducts. Henry's library consisted of his favourite Dale

Carnegie, four volumes of Churchill's *History of the Second World War* (given him as they came out by Mrs Lambert; unlike his godmother, he, an admirer of the war leader, had expressed a desire to have them; they remained unread). *The Nicomachean Ethics* of Aristotle (the books on friendship had attracted him but he had got no further than the chapter headings), *Look Down in Mercy*, *Giovanni's Room*, *Teach Yourself Book-keeping* and *Teach Yourself Mathematics*. His most valued possession was his record player and a number of long-play records, half vocal and half concert orchestra. Henry liked Harry Belafonte and was much taken with Guy Lombardo's 'sweetest music this side of heaven' – the tag appealed to him.

Henry was unresentful of the fact that Mrs Lambert had not left him more; he had no expectations. The hasty sale of Gorsebanks and the price James accepted had shocked him, but he admired James. With pride Henry talked of, 'My cousin, ever so wealthy and educated,' and when James had a novel published Henry saw that it was in the library of every ship in the fleet. 'The librarian's a friend of mine,' he told James. He'll do anything I ask.'

*

After three happy years in Japan, James returned to England. Finding that neither Florence's bungalow in Bournemouth, nor Donald's exiguous Ealing flat was adequate as a base, he bought the lease of a sizeable apartment in Kensington jointly with his lifelong friend. The arrangement suited Donald as well as it did James. Donald was now a lecturer at a London college and welcomed having spacious and central quarters. In making the arrangement James forgot about Henry.

It was not until James was staying with Florence in the summer of 1960, just before the removal of the Gorsebanks furniture to London from Bournemouth repository that he realised how much he had hurt Henry. The head waiter appeared unannounced one day soon after lunch. His ship was on cruises and had docked at Southampton.

'It's a quick turnaround,' he explained. 'I must get back tonight.'

'Can't you stay?' asked James, who was occupying the only spare room in the bungalow.

'Must get back. I have a lot to do before we sail tomorrow afternoon.'

The two men took themselves off for a walk along the cliff paths.

Henry said, 'I'm amazed, James.'

'What do you mean?'

'I thought we were going to share a place together when you came home.'

'I'm going away again. In any case you haven't left the sea. This place in London with Donald is only a base for me to go to when I'm in England.'

They waited until there was a gap between the queues of cars nose-tailing along the Overcliff Drive, and then crossed to the cliffs.

'I must say it was a shock when your aunt told me last week.'

'I'm sorry, but...' James stopped himself from saying that he had never promised to share a place with Henry; he had only said that he would help him if he went into business.

'What am I going to do with the furniture from my room at Gorsebanks that's in store with yours?'

'Keep it in store. Don't worry about it. I'll pay the dues. There simply isn't room for it in the London flat. I have to get rid of a lot of stuff as it is. I kept far too much.'

They walked along the asphalt paths in silence. The shelters were mostly occupied on this sunny, blustery day in July. Dogs sniffed each other in the marram grass, ignoring their owners' gruff commands. They went to the edge of the cliff. Henry put on a hand his head to hold his locks in place. He was pallid, having that pasty, indoor look of one who spends his time between decks breathing second-hand air; there were signs of wear such as crow's feet and lines on his forehead, yet, at thirty-five he was still a good-looking man.

Florence in her old age became quite a cordial to Henry. He attributed this to the fact that he went down to Bournemouth in a hired car and took her out for drives or to somewhere she wanted to visit.

'Have you brought a car?' she would ask before he had sat down. 'I wonder if you'd mind taking me to those nurseries on the other side of Christchurch. Henry never stayed with her although she invited him to – she was lonely; instead, he stayed with Mrs Jackson, whose nursing-home had been next to Gorsebanks and was now converted into flatlets. She had met Henry as a boy when he had paid his first visit to Mrs Lambert and she had liked him; he had always been pleasant to her. Readily she accepted his request to rent one of her rooms, which he had furnished with the contents of his old bedroom at Gorsebanks.

*

James spent the winter in Beirut and Cairo. Donald, solitary rather than gregarious, did not mind being alone in the large London flat. Alec had disappeared; he did not answer letters. By the following spring James was back in Tokyo.

*

Henry ruled the first-class dining-room with ability and charm; the passengers liked him and his subordinates respected him, at least most of them did. Some, those with whom Henry had been firm, carped at him behind his back, taking out their annoyance on Frank, who, since his promotion from tourist to first class had been indecently sudden, was known as 'mother's boy'. Notwithstanding, Frank was not the perfect lover. Henry adored him and suffered tortures of jealously when at ports, instead of accepting an invitation to spend the day with him, he went off with normal mates to hostess bars. Occasionally, when he was broke, Frank would consent to go ashore with Henry. One of the latter's great moments was when took his friend to a night club in Sydney that called itself the 'Home of the Elite' and the 'Choice of the Shrewd'. They had two bottles of champagne with their meal and listened to a super band with an American singer, whom the compere introduced as being famous in all five continents, although neither of them had heard of her. Henry was proud to take the beautiful Frank to this exclusive place and while there he was in an euphoric state, which the champagne was not entirely responsible for.

On another visit to Sydney (Henry knew Cliff's address but did not bother to look him up) Henry rented a car and made one of the cardinal errors of the enamoured: he let his lover drive. Frank, a reckless driver with no licence, ran off the road into a tree, and while, miraculously, the two friends were unharmed, the damage to the car was considerable, as was the sum Henry had to fork out to pay for it. Frank felt so contrite during the homeward voyage he became exceptionally co-operative, visiting the head waiter's private cabin regularly. The restaurant went well, the chief steward and the purser were easy to work with; there were few complaints. Henry was so pleased to hear Frank's knock on his cabin door about an hour after the second sitting for dinner that he willingly poured out liberal measures of whisky and opened a fresh packet of king-size cigarettes. It was not until two weeks had elapsed that he realised then he and Frank were consuming nearly a bottle a night. He wouldn't save much on this voyage, but he'd make up for it on the next, which was to be a long one to the Far East, Hawaii and the west coast of the United States. The company had decided to profit by the increasing Pacific trade, carrying Americans, who found English prices reasonable and British ships 'quaint', to Japan, to Manila, to Hong Kong, to Bangkok.

*

At the end of a long voyage stewards like sailors are tempted to have at least one wild night out. Henry was no exception. He persuaded Frank to spend the night with him at the Piccadilly Hotel. At breakfast time on their first morning at the hotel Henry rang Room Service and ordered coffee, croissants and a bottle of champagne.

'Champagne? You ordered champagne?' asked Frank, amazed.

'The best time to drink champagne is in the morning,' said Henry, loftily.

The waiter nearly dropped the tray bearing the breakfast and the champagne in surprise when he saw the two men in the double-bed together. 'Shall I open the wine, sir?' he asked.

'We can do that, thanks,' said Henry, adding when the waiter had gone after a throwing a quizzical regard from the door. 'You can do it, Frank; after all it's your job.'

'Right sir,' said Frank.

'They drank the champagne and ate the croissants, leaving the coffee which they agreed didn't go with the wine, and in a hilarious mood went off to lunch at the Jardin des Gourmets.

Before Frank went to see his family in Oxford the head waiter and the wine steward spent one more night at the Piccadilly Hotel, dining at the Ivy, where Frank was the cynosure of several pairs of old male eyes and sitting in the stalls at an American musical.

Henry drove down to Bournemouth in a hired car, stayed at Mrs Jackson's and took Florence out for a drive.

He hated the rest of his holiday; he was pained by thoughts of Frank with his family and with girls, or worse, with one girl. He longed to return to the ship, to the closed environment in which Frank was his, or, at least, nobody else's. Bournemouth was so dull, but he had nowhere else to go; he was even grateful to Florence for being there. 'Oh Henry,' she would say, 'would you mind taking my Foxy out?' Henry walked slowly up to the cliffs stopping at lamp posts for the little Cairn. 'Oh Henry, would you mind washing up the lunch things? It's Mrs Taylor's afternoon off;' 'Oh Henry, there's that stuff in the garage to be taken to the jumble sale.' 'Oh Henry…' The 'Oh Henrys' went on all the week and inwardly Henry groaned at each of them; he would have missed them if there had not been any. They made him feel wanted.

Florence was pleased when Henry came to Bournemouth; his presence made a change from her society of ancient ladies, as did the motor rides.

'If you're calling at Yokohama, you'll be seeing James, perhaps,' she said to Henry on the last day of his leave. 'Do find out what keeps him in Japan. Are the Japs so fascinating? Has he found a Madame Butterfly? I hope he doesn't marry a Japanese.'

*

'You'll like my cousin,' Henry told Frank as they were approaching Yokohama. 'Got real class, he has.'

James was waiting on the quay, impatient at the unconscionable time the huge, white ship took to dock, and then, when the Yokohoma brass band had played a welcome march and the gangways were put in place, he still had to wait until the disembarking passengers had gone ashore. Henry was nowhere to be seen. A regiment of black uniformed schoolboys and girls in dark blue dresses with sailor collars, who had been to watch the liner arrive, marched off. Sight-seeing buses filled up and moved away. Voyagers of independent spirit browsed around the temporary souvenir shops before setting off on their own to visit the city of Yokohama, which, apart from department stores and girlie bars, had little to offer the tourist. Soon a posse of the ship's crew wearing pullovers and slacks slouched off, hands in pockets, to spend the day in bars with diminutive yet business-like hostesses. At last, Henry, elegant and handsome in his uniform with two gold rings on the sleeves, appeared at the top of the gangway.

'You might have poked your nose out,' James complained. 'I've been waiting for hours.'

'Just couldn't, James. Haven't had a moment. Had all the seating to arrange in the dining-room. I've fixed a table for you for lunch. A table to yourself. You'd prefer that, wouldn't you?'

'Much. Aren't you coming in to Tokyo?'

'After lunch, James.'

'I've got tickets for Kabuki.'

'What's that?'

'Japanese theatre. Most spectacular. It begins at four-thirty.' James loved Kabuki and once a week sat through the long-winded plays as enthralled as a child at its first pantomime, although he understood less than one word in twenty. Since he had become a devotee of Kabuki, he could not imagine anyone being bored by it.

'I must be back by midnight,' said Henry leading the way to his cabin.

There was only one chair, a basket one, in the exiguous cabin and in it James was invited to sit. While Henry was pouring generous measures of gin, James glanced at the plaster heads of 'Prince' Monolulu, the Mexican peasant and the Red Indian chieftain, thinking how incongruous they looked above the bunk on either side of the familiar, golden framed triptych. It occurred to him for the first time, since he had never bothered to consider the matter before, that his mother's protégé was devoid of taste.

'You see I've got that picture up,' said Henry, as if he had read James's thoughts. He handed James a glass of gin and tonic. 'I'm afraid my man's forgotten the lemon.'

'Your man?'

'One of the Goanese waiters looks after me. I pay him of course.'

Henry's frequent glances at his watch made him seem on edge. 'I shall have to go down to the dining-room in a minute. You'll see Frank. I'll send him over to you. He's a wine steward. Order what you like. Frank can't come with us to Tokyo this afternoon. I've asked him for a drink tomorrow evening. You'll come to dinner, won't you? We sail at midnight. Like some music?' Henry slipped off his bed and sorted through some records stacked behind the player at James's side on the dressing table. Soon the oily voice of Johnny Mathis accompanied their conversation. Henry talked about Frank and of Florence, not of any of the places the ship had called at.

'I shall have to leave you now. Come down in half an hour. There's only one sitting as we're in port. If you want another drink or a record, help yourself.' He popped a pill into his mouth.

'What's that for?'

'My breath. I mustn't breathe gin into my passengers' faces.'

When Henry had gone, James switched off Johnny Mathis's pretentious mouthings of the idiocies of 'I've grown accustomed to your face,' and looked around for something to read. He came across the Complaints Book. It had entries in Henry's boyish hand.:

'Mrs Matthews of Cabin 351,' he read, 'complained that the liver she was served was not calves' liver but pigs' liver. I made enquiries in the galley and the chef informed me there was no pigs' liver on the ship. I told Mrs Mathews this but she insisted that she had been served pigs' liver. I suggested she had a steak. She agreed and was satisfied. H.H.'

Another entry concerned a Miss Johnson who had grumbled about feeling terribly bored during the wait between the end of the first sitting until Bingo began after the second sitting. 'I arranged for her to change to the second sitting. She was satisfied. H.H.'

✱

The Englishness of the dining-room made James feel he had been spirited home. Japan, although just outside the port-hole, seemed very distant. With professional correctness Henry conducted him to a table, handed him a menu, and with an authoritative air summoned a waiter.

'Don't forget to order what you like,' said Henry.

James did so. In a few minutes a young man with well-kept hands proffered the wine list.

'Like some wine, sir?'

James took off his reading glasses and glanced at Frank's radiant face. James was impressed. He put his spectacles back on his nose and perused the wine list.

'Please may I have a half bottle of Cotes du Rhone 1959? That was a good year.'

'Was it, sir?'

When he brought the wine, Frank said brightly, 'Thanks for telling me that '59 was a good year. It's useful for me to know something like that.'

He opened the bottle, poured a little into the glass and James went through the pantomime of tasting it. 'All right, sir?'

'Yes, thanks.'

'Thank you, sir.'

James found it hard to keep his eyes from following Frank all over the dining-room for the rest of the meal.

*

'What did you think? asked Henry.

James and he were hurtling towards Tokyo in the suburban train. When Henry had seen the packed carriages he had hesitated, giving a little flap with his long-fingered hand. 'We can't get into this.'

'Of course we can. Come on! Push!'

'What did you think of him? repeated Henry to James over the head of a female passenger who stood between them.

'Very fine. He doesn't know much about wine, though.'

'No need to. The only French wine most passengers have heard of is Beaujolais.'

Henry fidgeted during the Kabuki performance, mistrusted both the *sake* and the raw tuna (which James loved) at the *sushi* bar and kept saying when they wandered through the foyers during an interval, 'What a crush of people everywhere, in the train, here in the theatre. Don't you get tired of it, James?' His only remark about the performance, which they left before the end, was, 'Very colourful, James, but so slow.'

After dinner on the ship the next evening, Frank joined Henry and James in the cabin. The young wine steward said little. He showed his fondness for liquor by gulping down the large whisky which Henry gave him and then held out his glass for another. Frank's answer to James's platitudinous questions – 'Where do you live in England? How do you like Japan? Which is your favourite port of call?' – were monosyllabic. After a third whisky, Frank said, politely, 'I expect you two have a lot to say to each other.' 'Don't go Frank,' pleaded Henry. Frank left.

When James got up to leave, Henry said, 'Can you find your way off the ship? D'you mind?'

James's eyebrows shot up to their highest level

'I've had too much to walk to the gangway. Don't want anyone to see.' Henry swayed a bit in the narrow gangway and clutched the handrail.

James's 'goodnight' was curt. He had not realised that Henry had knocked back so much whisky.

In the train back to Tokyo, James composed a censorious letter, which he planned to send to Henry's next port of call: Hong Kong.

*

The sting of James's avuncular letter was alleviated by the arrival on board at Colombo of Lord Rodmell. His Lordship had a good memory and while he could not remember Henry's name, he recognised him at once. Tactfully he evinced no surprise that the 'wealthy provincial businessman,' a fellow member of the Beckford, was now a head waiter. In compliance with a request sent in advance to the ship by the agent, Henry had arranged for the peer to have a table to himself.

In the dining-room Godfrey Rodmell spoke discreetly to Henry, who was obsequious, piling on the 'my lords' with the proverbial trowel. On his way out of the dining-room after his first dinner on board, Rodmell asked Henry about Frank, who had attended to his order for wine.

'That wine waiter of yours?' he asked. 'Is he er...'

'No, but after a few drinks he'll play.'

'I'd like to meet him.'

'I think I can fix that,' boasted Henry, anxious to please and to impress.

Godfrey Rodmell, second baron, was now over sixty. His shining bald crown was bordered by a hedge of gray; his face was still ruddy, his hacking smoker's cough remained unconquered and his suave, confident manner had not diminished. In the years between seeing Henry at the Beckford and meeting him on the liner, he had become a prominent member of the Labour Party.

Henry invited the peer to his cabin after the second sitting the following evening. It being the second night out passengers in first class were expected to dress. Rodmell looked grand and distinguished in his well-cut dinner jacket. Henry's quarters being in the passengers' section of the ship were not difficult to find, nevertheless Henry's guest had to ask the way of several stewards, one of whom led him to the cabin and smiled at the head waiter when he opened the door.

'Thank you so much,' said Rodmell to the steward, nodding courteously.

Nervously, Henry shut the door and offered the one chair to Rodmell, who said, puffing at his cigar, 'What about you?'

'Please,' insisted Henry. 'I'll sit on the bunk. What will you have to drink my lord?'

'Oh, no 'my lords'. Godfrey, please. And you are –'

'Henry.'

'Oh yes, of course. Those Beckford days were so long ago. I didn't know you were in the Merchant Navy.'

'My business didn't do well. I joined again. I was at sea before.'

'Do you like it? It's not bad to be head waiter first class, and with a cabin to yourself.' There was a pause before Godfrey said, 'Is that charming wine waiter coming?'

'He'll be along soon. He has to help clear up and lay the table for breakfast. A whisky, my lord – I mean Godfrey.'

'I'd love one.'

Henry rose from the bunk and deftly poured out two stiff whiskies, adding ice and a dash of water. 'Here's luck,' he said.

'Thanks.'

'I wonder why you don't fly,' said Henry.

'I like a sea voyage,' replied the peer. 'It's restful and now the Canal's open again the trip isn't too long. I'm disembarking at Marseilles anyway.'

There came a knock on the door and Frank appeared.

'This is Frank Reid,' said Henry. Please meet Lord...'

The peer rose. 'Godfrey Rodmell,' he said, shaking hands with Frank. 'It's good to meet informally.'

Frank sat on the bunk. Henry poured him a whisky.

'How did you like Ceylon, I mean Sri Lanka?' asked Godfrey.

'Only ever seen a bit of Colombo,' replied Frank. 'Not much of a place. The people look so dirty and they spit blood on the pavement.'

'It's not blood, my dear,' corrected the peer. 'It's the juice of the betel nut, which they chew, and they're not dirty. They're cleaner than we are, really.'

'They don't look it.' Frank spoke naturally with no hint of deference. 'What were you doing in Sri Lanka?'

'I went there for a rest and also...'

'You don't have to work, do you?

'I'm kept quite busy doing Party – Labour – Work. Apart from having a change there were three reasons for my visiting Ceylon, I mean Sri Lanka. When one has been used to calling a country by its old name, its hard to remember to call it by its new one.'

'Like with people,' put in Frank, who seemed keen to hold his own with the peer. 'I knew someone called Stanley and he hated it. He started to call himself Stephen and got angry when anyone called him Stanley.'

Godfrey laughed politely. Frank downed his whisky in one gulp. Rodmell, after emitting a series of wheezy coughs continued. 'My three reasons for visiting Ceylon were: looking up the High Commissioner, who is a friend of mine, staying with a chum on his tea plantation and seeking out a school acquaintance, who seems to have gone native – his sister asked me to find out about him. He's become a Buddhist and lives a life of meditation in the jungle. His father was an earl and died recently; he inherited the title.'

Godfrey mainly addressed Frank, giving just an occasional glance at Henry, who was beginning to wonder if he'd done the right thing in introducing his friend to the peer; he had wanted to impress and at the same time boost his own morale. 'May I refill your glass, Godfrey?' Henry rose from the stool he had pulled out from under the washbasin.

'That would be kind.'

Henry poured fresh drinks and Godfrey went on: 'Well, when a message got through to the meditating monk in the midst of the jungle that his father was dead, he made one of his rare visits to the High Commission in Colombo and had his new title entered into his passport. The High Commissioner was much amused. He thought that having become a religious recluse he would renounce all worldly possessions and titles.' Godfrey laughed. The others smiled weakly.

'What about the money he got when his father died?' asked Henry.

'The estate apart from an allowance, went to his brother. One wonders if he'll tire of his life of abnegation and rejoin society.'

'Does he live alone under the trees?' asked Frank in a slightly mocking tone.

'He's in a temple, which he restored, and there are a few other monks with him,' replied Godfrey seriously.

'You didn't see him?' asked Frank.

'I sent a message and a reply eventually came saying he didn't want to see me. I wasn't sorry. The temple is remote and it required a jungle trek with a guide. It is on the east coast, where trouble is brewing with the Tamils. The Tamils are mostly Hindu, while the Singalese are...' Godfrey noticed that Henry and Frank were no longer listening. He ceased his rigmarole and said, 'I'm boring you. Sorry.'

'No, do go on,' pleaded Henry. 'You said that the Singalese were...'

'Mostly Buddhist.'

'Lets have some music,' suggested Frank.

Henry put on a selection from *Hello, Dolly*.

'Dear Mary Martin,' mused Godfrey. 'I shall always remember her singing on the first night. "Hello London, it's so nice to be back in Drury Lane", when the first time she was at that theatre it was in that ghastly flop, *Pacific 1860* by Coward. Poor Noel!' These reminiscences of the peer bought no reaction from the young men. Godfrey would have liked to have been asked if he knew Coward, which he did. The familiar songs from the musical comedy were listened to in silence. When they were over, Godfrey rose. 'I must go to bed,' he announced. 'You've been very generous with your whisky, Henry. Thank you so much. He opened the door. 'I'm not sure that I can find my way,' he said giving Frank a look.

Frank, who was on his feet, said, 'I'll show you.'

'You oughtn't to go to that part of the ship,' Henry warned his friend.

'Fuck that,' retorted Frank and he left the cabin with the peer.

*

Henry was miserable. Frank hadn't paid his customary after-dinner visits to his cabin for several evenings. He suspected he was seeing Godfrey Rodmell and he cursed himself for having introduced him to the peer. Henry regarded himself in the looking-glass. James' letter admonishing him about drinking too much had no effect, in fact it had merely annoyed him. Careful perusal of his face told him that he looked tired, his eyes were dull, his cheeks pale, but surely he was more attractive than that bloated lord.

Many a working-class or lower middle class lad is impressed by a title, and, like Henry, Frank was no exception.

'You're seeing Godfrey Rodmell,' Henry challenged Frank one evening between dinner settings.

'What if I am?'

'You might come and see me.'

'I'll look in some time, maybe.'

Henry was hurt by this offhand reply. As regards the peer, he had spoken cordially to Henry when there was an opportunity during lunch or dinner, but he made no mention of Frank and Henry did not dare ask if the young wine waiter was visiting him.

After the second sitting of dinner, Henry would go back to his cabin and brood, and while moping he drank large measures of whisky. This indulgence became a habit and more than once the chief steward noticed the unsteady state he was in and warned him. Two passengers had complained to the chief steward of Henry's smelling of alcohol and forgetting requests. Henry's drinking became so bad that one morning he was scarcely able to cope with his duties. He tottered about to the amusement of some passengers, but to the embarrassment and fury of the chief steward, who ordered his wretched, unhappy head waiter to return to his cabin and report sick. The ship's doctor saw at once what was the matter and sent him to the sick bay, where he was put on a course of detoxicants; he was not allowed to resume his duties.

Just before Lord Rodmell disembarked at Marseilles he asked Frank about Henry and was told he was in trouble having hit the bottle too hard. The peer asked the chief steward, who told him that Henry was ill and could see no one.

'But I *want* to see him,' insisted the peer.

'I'll ask the doctor, my lord.'

In the confusion and haste of disembarkation Rodmell managed to see Frank, to whom he gave two envelopes: one containing a generous tip for him and the other a similar gift for Henry, whom he had been unable to see. He had not liked to push his request.

On the ship's arrival at London Henry was dismissed, and Frank, thinking it unwise to be associated with him, gave Rodmell's present to the chief steward to pass on to Henry. Frank went home to Oxford, where he spent his leave with his family; when it was over he rejoined the ship. He did not contact Henry.

Meanwhile Henry loaded his belongings into a hired car and drove to Mrs Jackson's in Bournemouth. Florence had died. She had not remembered him in her will.

Part V

With his severance pay from the shipping company, his savings in the Trustee Savings Bank, Henry had just over £5000. What was he to do? There seemed to be no occupation available in England except that of a waiter in a restaurant or in a supermarket stacking shelves. Both demeaning jobs after running the first class dining-room on a famous ship. James was in Tokyo. There was no one he could go to for advice. He thought of writing to Lord Rodmell, whom he had never thanked for his tip, but the peer at home in his grand milieu did not seem approachable as he had been on the ship. Henry wrote to Cliff in Sydney asking if he'd like some help, adding that he had a few thousand he could put into Cliff's business. Cliff replied by return and asked Henry to join him as soon as possible, suggesting that Henry become his partner. His offer was tempting.

*

Cliff's uncle had died, leaving his nephew the hotel, a small establishment in Paddington, a district in Sydney of Victorian style houses. The hotel consisted of three terraced houses converted into one building. The uncle had been predeceased by his wife and his sole offspring, a daughter, had married and gone to live in Perth. She had shown no interest in the hotel until her father's death. Her husband learnt from his lawyer, whom he sent to Sydney, to investigate the situation, that the place was heavily mortgaged and would prove to be an expensive liability. 'Leave well alone,' he advised his wife. 'Let that drunken pansy stew in his own mess.'

*

'How much can you let me have, ducks?' Cliff asked Henry when at last the arrival procedure was over and they were on the motorway from the airport to Sydney.

'What do you mean?' said Henry, astonished that Cliff should ask for money before they had even reached the hotel.

'Well, you said you'd agree to become my partner and in a partnership both partners put something into the business.'

'How's the hotel doing?'

'Business is a bit slow at the moment. It will pick up I'm sure. This hotel is in a very desirable district that's becoming distinctly upmarket…'

'What's the problem then?'

'My uncle ran the place into debt. It'll be a hell of a job getting things right.'

'How many guests do you have?'

'Two.'

'Two? Only two? And staff?'

'One. He does everything: the rooms, the shopping, the cooking. He's Chinese.'

Henry, who had been full of expectation and optimism about a new future with a 'new Cliff', felt despondent and depressed. A different Cliff rather than a 'new' one. Cliff looked his age, which was verging on sixty. Henry guessed why Cliff smelt of peppermint in the car; he knew about menthol tablets to kill alcoholic breath; he had often taken them before going on duty after drinking in his cabin. His suspicions were confirmed on arrival at the hotel. It was only 9 a.m. when Cliff showed Henry into what he called his office, a sitting-room with armchairs and a large table strewn with letters, some opened, some still sealed; on the table was a half-empty bottle of Scotch. Cliff said, 'Have a drink, ducks! After that flight I guess you need one.'

'I've given up,' Henry admitted.

'Christ, I wish I had.'

'But you did give up.'

'For a while I did. My uncle drank. He broke down my resistance. It wasn't very strong anyway. And so…' Cliff shrugged.

'May I look round.'

Cliff poured out a stiff measure of whisky into a used glass. 'You have a good look at the place. I'll rest a bit. Had to get up at sparrow fart to meet you.'

Henry soon saw that the hotel needed a thorough refurbishment, which he reckoned would cost more than the few thousand he had.

*

Henry had never found orientals attractive; but when he met Cliff's cook in the kitchen on his tour of the hotel; he was at once drawn to him. The cook was sitting at the kitchen table looking at the television. He got up when Henry entered the room. He smiled broadly and held out a hand which Henry took in his and held longer than is usual at first meeting, and looked into the dark Chinese eyes.

'I'm Henry Harlow.'

'I know. Cliff he tell me you coming. My name is Ken Yeo. Call me Ken.'

Henry sat at the table and Ken opposite him in his previous place.

After a silence, Henry said, 'How are things?'

'Bad. This hotel no good. Cliff he drink all the time. He do nothing, jus' drink.'

'Why do you stay?'

'Criff he guarantee me for residence. Mus' stay till I get residence. He kind to me. Took me in. I can't reave him.'

'And then?'

'I wan' open restaurant, Chinese style. Have no money.'

Henry rose. Ken got up too. He was nearly as tall as Henry. Instead of leaving the room at once to continue his tour of the hotel, Henry moved towards him, looked into his eager eyes; in a moment they were in each others arms and kissing deeply.

'You gay?' asked Ken 'I gay, I li' you.'

They kissed some more.

Henry broke away, swallowed, took a breath and murmured, 'We must talk things over.'

'More than jus' talk,' replied Ken, emitting a shrill chuckle.

*

James, still in Tokyo, received a letter from Henry with a New South Wales postmark. He assumed that Henry's ship was on a cruise to Australia and he was surprised to learn that Henry had left the sea and was helping an

old shipmate run a hotel in Sydney. 'There are great opportunities here',
Henry wrote. 'The hotel could be made into a goldmine if money were
spent on it. I'm really onto a good thing. With fifteen thousand this place
could become one of the best small hotels in Sydney. I swear it could. I'm
going to invest all my savings in the business. If you could put up ten
thousand – you promised you'd help me start a business when I left the
sea – it would be wonderful. It would be a loan of course. I would pay
you interest. James, I know I can make a go of this. It's the chance of a
lifetime. I've had lots of experience in catering and managing a dining
room and in business...'

There was no mention of his partner in the letter, and after all ten
thousand pounds was a lot of money. James replied that he couldn't send
such a large amount at once, but would ask his bank in England to send
two thousand pounds. In fact James, who was saving half his generous
salary from the Japanese university that employed him, could easily have
afforded the requested sum. His shrewd financial adviser in London had
impressively increased his capital and he did not need to touch his private
income. He surmised, wrongly, that Henry had asked for much more than
he needed and anyway he would probably squander the money and ask
for more. Why had Henry left the sea? Was he now mixed up in a racket?
His previous attempts at business had ended in failure. What a nuisance his
mother's protégé was! James wished that his father hadn't taken the dogs
for a walk on that fatal day. He realised that his parents' act of charity had
been well meant; however, James decided that it had done more harm
than good. Mrs Lambert had thought she had helped Henry. James wasn't
sure that her allowing Henry to regard Gorsebanks as his home had made
him envious of him, and introduced a way of life he could not easily attain
on his own. Henry might have been happier if he had not known the
Lamberts and like other Home boys settled for a modest job. His desire
for riches had led to disaster, James thought. James was sure that his new
venture would come to nothing.

*

'You've had it off with Ken, haven't you?' said Cliff to Henry, a week or
so later.

'How do you know?' asked Henry, on the defensive.

'You were not in your room when I went along the passage to the toilet last night.'

Henry said nothing.

'I don't mind. I've had him enough times. We only did it because we were both sex starved. And he had an ulterior motive: to get me to back him for a residence permit, which I did. He's Chinese, don't forget. I'm through with sex now. Can't get it up anymore.' Cliff paused. It was nearly noon. They were sitting at the table in the office. A half-full glass of whisky stood before Cliff, who was wearing an unironed shirt and crumpled trousers. 'I thought you weren't turned on by "chinks," went on Cliff. 'Especially gay ones. You always liked straight English boys.'

In reply Henry said, 'Ken's different somehow. I think I'm in love.'

'Love!' Cliff exclaimed, derisively. 'I admit though the Chinese are good at it. They take it more serious-like than we do. But Ken is very much a man, you know.'

'I know. He fits somehow. This morning Ken and I were discussing the possibilities of this place.'

'Excluding me, I suppose.' Cliff's bloodshot eyes blazed. 'You can't get rid of me.' He banged the table with his fist. The whisky danced in the glass.

'Ken's keen to start a restaurant and I –'

'He's been on about turning this place into a restaurant ever since he's been here. Where's the money coming from?' Cliff took a swig of whisky. 'You said you'd put up something.'

'Five thousand pounds and maybe a bit more,' James had not yet sent any money.

'I need more to pay my debts, ducky. I think I'd better sell the fucking place.'

'Then what'll I do?'

'I could ask the same question about myself, lovey.'

∗

Henry wrote another letter to James in Tokyo asking if could send the promised two thousand pounds, and if he could manage five or ten it would really set him firmly on his feet, and of course he would pay James back once the business was making some money. He explained that he, his friend Cliff and a Chinese were planning to start a restaurant and capital was needed urgently. Henry's letter ended with, 'I know I am onto a good thing. Please help. You won't regret it.' James's reply was not encouraging; he did though, say he'd send five thousand.

Meanwhile Cliff, Henry and Ken busied themselves with preparations for the restaurant, Cliff's efforts mostly consisted of impractical suggestions that were disregarded and promises that were never kept. He was, nevertheless, helpful over contacts which Ken or Henry took up. Ken and Henry got on well as business partners and in bed. Ken saw to it that business came first. The hotel side of the business was terminated. The two guests had to be paid to leave owing to promises Cliff had given them.

Weeks went by, vicissitudinous weeks of construction and frustration. It was better that Cliff continued to hit the bottle; his drunken state prevented him from interfering with the alterations. He would throw a fit of temper over a plan devised by Ken and Henry saying it was impossible and then would abandon his objection and allow it to be executed – 'Oh all right,' he would say. 'You know best, I suppose, but I have my doubts.'

Eventually and with much trepidation on Ken's and Henry's account, the restaurant opened. After a desperate letter from Henry, James relented and sent ten thousand pounds and the bank granted a loan. The name of the restaurant had caused much contention. Ken wanted it to be called Ken's Chinese Place. Cliff favoured Cliff's Restaurant. Henry had no say; he supported Ken. Finally Cliff gave in.

With Ken in the kitchen, Henry in charge of the dining-room the business began promisingly. Ken got hold of some Chinese immigrants from Hong Kong to work in the kitchen and in the dining-room. Cliff, now in a dire state, rarely rose from his bed upstairs. Henry became the general manager.

Henry was happy in Australia. His origins, in the almost classless society, were unimportant. For the first time in his life he had shed his inferiority complex; no chips remained on his shoulders. At the end of two years he was able to pay James £1000. It pleased him to do so, but it annoyed Ken. The altercation about the remittance to James blew over, none the less Henry felt it continue to rankle.

'Mus' you pay back money to your cousin?' asked Ken of Henry one night when they were in bed together.'

'It was a loan, Ken, I promised to pay it back, bit by bit.'

'We not made much profit. We need to implove the place more. Kitchen mus have new fligerator.'

'It was a gesture to show willing. To show we're doing well. It's important for me to show James we're successful.'

'I see,' said Ken, after thought. 'What abou' me?'

'Well, it's no less important to you, is it?'

✳

The years passed. Ken's Chinese Place prospered. Cliff died leaving the restaurant to Henry and Ken jointly.

Ken in his spotless chef's outfit, his tall white hat at a slight angle, had an impish regard. Once or twice an evening he would emerge from the kitchen and tour the tables, stealing a little of Henry's thunder. Henry with a carnation or a rose in his dinner-jacket's lapel would welcome customers and summon a waiter to attend to them. His dignified charm was one of the reasons for the restaurant's success, and the cooking of course was another. Ken's reputation as a chef was enhanced by his giving demonstrations on the Chinese cuisine on television; Henry became a well-known restaurateur. The success was mainly due to Ken's determination and diligence; it was he who saw that Henry concentrated on his job and did not seek diversions elsewhere. Ken did not allow sex to interfere with business. Work came first.

Henry honoured his debt to James. This pleased the latter and at the same time embarrassed him. The return of the loan, though gradual, made James's promise to help Henry when he left the sea seem empty. James felt that his ace had been trumped. In an effort to temper his feeling of guilt he told himself that he had not asked Henry to pay interest.

✳

In 1978 James, now tubby, hair thanks to Trumpers' 'restorer' not very grey, was sixty. He now had a permanent contract with the Tokyo university and was happily settled in a reasonably sized apartment (for Tokyo) in a pleasant and convenient district. Since direct flights to England had started he spent the summer vacation with Donald Dawson in their London flat. Communication with Henry had except for a

135

Christmas card with a brief message dried up. The previous year's message from Henry read, 'Happy Christmas and all that. Business fine, Ken fine, me fine, love Henry.' Against Donald's advice, James decided at the beginning of his 61st year to end his summer vacation with a visit to Sydney.

'Great mistake,' Donald said. 'I don't think Henry would really want to see you. He may pretend to but he'd rather not. He's started a new life and wants to forget the past.'

'I'm curious to see his set-up.'

'A selfish curiosity,' remarked Donald. 'And there's that embarrassment over that money, which you should have given, not lent, him.'

'That's all forgotten,' said James.

'Don't you believe it. Money matters of that kind never are.'

James warned Henry of his proposed visit and asked him to arrange accommodation in Sydney.

'We put him in hotel,' said Ken firmly.

'He could stay here,' objected Henry.

'Hotel better. We too busy have visitor.'

'We had your parents from Hong Kong here.'

'Not same.'

Henry gave in as he invariably did. Perhaps Ken was right. James would require less looking after if he were in a hotel.

At first James didn't recognise Henry among the welcomers at Sydney airport. It was Henry who came up to James pushing his luggage trolley. 'Hello, James!'

'Why Henry!'

Henry, wearing smart casual clothes, looked so different. His hair had receded, his face had lined, but his air of prosperity and confident manner were the main causes of change that had taken place in him. He took over James's trolley and soon they were in a Mercedes heading towards the city.

'Is this your car?' James foolishly asked.

'It's our car, Ken's and mine. Did you think it was stolen?'

'Of course not. The restaurant must be doing well.'

'Yes, we're doing not quite bad, as Ken would say. I hope you don't mind staying in a hotel James. There's not much room in our place and we're both busy most of the time. Ken's arranged for one of his cousins to show you around.'

James was taken to a five star hotel near the quay. 'I'll call you,' said Henry. 'I have to go back to the restaurant and get ready for the evening.'

'Can't you lunch with me?' asked James. He wasn't hungry after the long flight but it was lunch time in Sydney.

'Sorry. Must rush. Have a nice stay! Bye!' Henry said after James had checked in at the front desk. He made for the exit and then came back as James was starting to follow the bellboy with his bags, 'By the way, James you're not to pay for anything in the hotel. It's all on us. Bye again.' Henry hurried away.

James lay on the king-size bed in his well appointed bedroom and wondered about Henry, this new Henry, who seemed a stranger. Was it Australia or the prosperity that had changed the orphan? James decided that growing up in the Home, where he had kindness up to a point but no love and Mrs Lambert's limited affection, his chequered career at sea, his brush with the motor trade, his loveless sex life had hardened him; after all James admitted to himself he hadn't shown Henry much warmth of friendship; he had treated him like a distant relation who had to be tolerated. James felt contrite and ashamed that he had not told Henry when he had sent him the £10,000 that it was a gift.

The telephone awoke James from a deep slumber. It was Henry to say that dinner would be difficult, but he would be sending his car to take him for a drive the next morning and then to the restaurant for lunch. Over dinner in the hotel restaurant James felt that Donald had been right. His coming to see Henry had been a mistake. The curt 'Bye!' more than anything had made James realise that Henry did not wish his past to impinge on his present. A fresh leaf had been turned with a vengeance. Before the car arrived the next morning to take him on a sightseeing tour, James booked a flight to Tokyo for the following day.

The driver, a cousin of Ken's, was deferential and dutiful and took Henry in the Mercedes to the Opera House, Darling Point and the mouth of the magnificent harbour before depositing him at Ken's Chinese Place, which only opened for business in the evening.

Conversation at the lunch, held in the empty restaurant, did not flow and was constantly interrupted by assistants wanting advice or approval for some action from either Henry or Ken, and when the three were alone the manager and the chef could not stop talking shop. James noticed that Henry usually agreed with an idea of Ken's which he at first had challenged. James, now accustomed to oriental features and liking them, found Ken appealing; by his manner, the way he regarded Henry, it was clear that he was devoted to him.

Not once did either of the two partners ask James about his life in Japan or his future plans. When at the end of the meal they rose from the table James bid Ken goodbye, 'I'm leaving tomorrow. I'm glad you've made a success of this place.'

'Thank you,' said Ken and disappeared into the region of the kitchen.

'You leaving so soon?' asked Henry.

'I must, I'm afraid.'

'There's so much I wanted to say.'

'Better left unsaid, perhaps.'

'What time's your plane to Japan?

'Early. I must be at the airport at eight.'

'I'll send the car,' said Henry.